An Authoress and a Viscount

Ann Hawthorne

Contents

Chapter 1

Lavinia wasn't sure what exactly she expected from this year, the third year of her service at court. Part of her hoped the rules would relax and a lively quadrille would be allowed into the mix of dances. But it was as foolish a hope as wishing the sun would rise in the west one day. As far as Her Majesty was concerned, all this skipping around and twirling was most improper and certainly would not do at a ball in her honour.

Lavinia had never been to a proper ball before she came to court as the second keeper of the robes. Not even at the height of her literary fame, when she was feted by the late Dr Johnson's own friends, did she receive such invitations. However, she was far from ignorant of the output of printers. Her publisher, Mr Wickman of St Paul's Churchyard, made a good trade of music sheets for quadrilles and, for the more staid dancers, allemandes.

But that was outside, in the bustling world of London and Bath and Bristol and the cities beyond – in the world where life was churning like a wild sea. Here, at King George's court, it was more akin to a mirror-smooth lake, and the dance seen most frequently at his queen's birthday balls was the cotillion. This year, like all others, Queen Charlotte's birthday ball was held before her birthday. Her birthday was in May; however, according to the labyrinthine logic of court ceremonies, her birthday was celebrated in January.

Lavinia drank her third glass of unsweetened champagne this evening. She was not usually partial to the drink – to any alcoholic drink – but it was hard to keep herself lively, or even lifelike, otherwise. She couldn't imagine where the tales of court leisure and indolence came from. Perhaps, this sort of life really was going on somewhere far away beyond the orbit of her own experience. Lavinia, however, had to get up at six in the morning today – just as she had to do yesterday and every morning for the three years before that – and patiently wait to be summoned to her duties. But, of course, she couldn't even show a hint of that kind of regimen at Queen Charlotte's birthday ball. She knew that these were her duties, too – to smile and pretend gentle joy.

Not just to pretend, she reminded herself. To be properly good and grateful, she had to do her best to feel it in her heart. How unnatural was she that an appointment most women in the country would have committed murder for brought her nothing but dull misery?

'This is going to be your last champagne flute for the evening,' Mrs Juliana Schwellenberg said, her tone that of a guardian to a child as opposed to merely the first keeper of the robes to her second. 'You have indulged yourself quite enough.'

'I had no intention of indulging myself,' Lavinia tried to explain in a voice as patient as it was deferential. 'It is only that I am a little tired, and—'

'Tired! What a fragile creature you are. One would have thought that women reared from your origins have hardier souls and bodies than this.'

Lavinia's father was a music tutor and a scholar, and her late mother was a harp prodigy. To listen to the court ladies, one might have thought Lavinia spent her childhood tilling hard soil.

She did not correct the older woman, however. That, she knew, would lead to nothing but further acrimony. She had to do the sensible thing. She had to swallow the implied insult, pretend she was too foolish to have understood it, and nod.

Loud laughter caught her attention. She was acquainted with the men laughing – the royal equerries, from the young ones to the old ones, but she knew none of them well. They were standing apart as a small group, all tall and broad shouldered – the young men strapping, the senior courtiers having the look of military heroes. All but the man who had just finished speaking, the one whose joke caused such uproarious laughter.

He was tall; however, that was the only thing the sandy-haired gentleman had in common with them. He was lithe rather than thickly muscular and dressed in the pink of fashion to a slightly greater extent than was acceptable at the strict and sober court of King George and Queen Charlotte. His formal waistcoat of white silk was embroidered a smidgen too elaborately; his shirt, as far as Lavinia could judge from its exquisitely ruffled sleeves, was also of silk instead of linen.

Among the other men, he seemed to glow, and it was not only the matter of the candlelight reflecting upon his pale-fair hair.

'God Almighty,' Mrs Schwellenberg said, 'in my day, a young man of his kind would have been called a macaroni.'

'Why?' Lavinia asked, not dragging her gaze away.

'Because of the Italian foppishness, of course. Though, I suppose, these days, most fops rather emulate the French.'

What a peculiar thing the Mrs Schwellenberg's mind must be, Lavinia mused, as must the mind of most courtiers be. Out in the streets, in the coffee houses and print shops of London, emulating the French meant alarming things that started with atheism and ended in a royal murder. Here, within the walls of St James Palace – or Kew, or, more usually, Windsor – time stood still, and the French ways still meant fashions and elaborate wigs.

The fair-haired equerry looked away from his friends and right at her. His eyes were grass green, and a smile of merriment was still on his lips. These were lips that some – Mrs Schwellenberg, for one – would have called uncommonly full for a man.

For a second, Lavinia imagined the devastation this smile and this mouth must have caused among the ladies of the ton before the gentleman took his honoured post and among the ladies of the court after he did.

'I do hope,' the first keeper of the robes remarked, 'you are not finding yourself enraptured by Viscount Granville.'

'Of course not.' Lavinia finally looked at her, but she couldn't quite summon enough indignation to infuse her voice with. 'I didn't even know his name and title before you told me.'

'I doubt you have any need to know his Christian name in any case. It is unlikely your paths are going to cross that often. At least, I hope they won't for the sake of your own safety.'

'Is he a violent man?'

'He is worse. He is a man without an earnest bone in his body as countless ladies who had been the recipients of his gallantry can attest. The ladies in question had their husbands' names to protect them, not to mention their noble blood. You, Miss Dudley, do not.'

Lavinia recoiled almost physically. The first keeper of the robes was often guilty of petty cruelty, but lying was not among her habits. If what Mrs Schwellenberg said was true, Lord Granville was one of the most dangerous creatures to young women like her. A pretty-coloured viper, someone apt to drain one's life and dignity away before leaving one as a disgraced husk and merrily moving along to another victim.

Lavinia wasn't sure vipers drained their victims. She made a mental note to work on her metaphors. Her new life of service gave her very little time for actual writing, but that didn't mean she could allow her skills to go to waste.

It was as though the viscount heard her thoughts, for as soon as the music had stopped, he stepped away from his group and walked in her direction. He couldn't be genuinely interested in her company, could he? The sandy-haired viscount stopped when he reached the corner where Lavinia and Mrs Schwellenberg were standing.

At first, Lavinia still entertained some vain hope he wanted to strike up a conversation with the first keeper of the robes, a far more exalted lady than Lavinia herself was or would ever be. When a smile lit up his face like a touch of sunlight, it was Lavinia he was looking at.

'I don't believe I had the honour of being introduced to you. I beg you to forgive me.' His voice was light as satin without a trace of any kind of grave regret. 'I haven't had the time to make many acquaintances. Serving His Majesty is not a sinecure.'

Neither is serving Her Majesty, Lavinia wanted to reply in this same easy, sparkling tone. His words loosened something in her, if only for a moment. That must have been how those women who followed every dictate of fashion and laced their waists in tightly felt when their stays were loosened.

But the first keeper of the robes was breathing over her shoulder, and the ballroom was filled with people with keen ears. So, Lavinia couldn't say the truth or even hint at it. Instead, she schooled her face into an expression of formal politeness and replied, 'I am sure it's a great honour for your family.'

'My father would have considered it a great honour indeed, had he still been with us.'

'His Majesty is a father to us all,' Mrs Schwellenberg intervened sharply. 'And he has need of his sons, especially in times of trouble.'

Lavinia suspected all three of them knew that when she spoke of trouble it was not the war with France she meant. It was the battle raging inside King George's own head, the battle where there could be no victors.

But no one speaks of such things in the middle of a glittering ballroom, guarded and warmed against the winter chill, on an occasion as awash with joy as a royal birthday. No one was supposed to.

'No doubt,' Lord Granville replied flippantly. 'Would you be so kind as to introduce one of his metaphorical sons to his metaphorical daughter, in that case?'

'Miss Dudley,' Mrs Schwellenberg said coldly, 'let me introduce Hugh, Viscount Granville to you. Your lordship, let me introduce to you Miss Lavinia Dudley, the second keeper of the robes.'

'Miss Dudley? The famed novelist?'

'That she might have been before she accepted Her Majesty's gracious offer. Now, she is the second keeper of the robes.'

'It would be a shame,' Lord Granville said, 'if one of these things really could supersede the other. My cousins were quite enraptured by *Miranda*.'

'I don't believe I know the lady,' the first keeper of the robes replied.

'*Miranda* was Miss Dudley's debut novel.'

'My only novel, so far,' Lavinia ventured, the old fear gripping her again. What if it was really to be her only novel? What if she never finished all those other frantic works she started and left after arriving at court – or what if she finished them but they produced nothing but disappointment in the reading public? That would almost be worse.

An unwritten work was always a masterpiece while a thing on paper was more often than not a misshapen clod of words.

'Modest as well as lovely,' Lord Granville observed. 'If I were a man writing for the papers, I would already be puffing you up on account of these things alone.'

'Your lordship, this is quite forward,' Mrs Schwellenberg said sharply.

'Is it? I am not commenting on the allure of her gown.'

'Presumably because you weren't raised in the gutter.'

'I do wonder if Miss Dudley would do me the honour of dancing with me?' He spoke as though the reproaches had never come and didn't pierce him the way they did Lavinia.

Lavinia knew she must not say yes to this man under any circumstances. But, God above, how dearly she wanted to. She knew in her bones this man would enliven even the stately cotillion even if he would never have a hand anywhere near her waist as he would have had in the allemande.

But she also knew she was not a woman of an iron willpower, that her reputation was a fragile thing, and above all, people were watching her for a misstep.

'Forgive me, your lordship,' Lavinia mumbled. 'But I feel unwell tonight and in no mood for dancing.'

'Do you? I am sorry to hear that. I imagine so would most men tonight.'

The implication was clear. If she used her transparent excuse, it would mean she would also have to forgo dancing altogether for this evening.

The smile on Lord Granville's lips remained just as charming.

'I am just as sorry to be disappointing them,' Lavinia said steadfastly, 'but such are the circumstances.'

'In that case, I would hate to impose my company on you. I wish you to enjoy the occasion.' He nodded to her and, as though it were an afterthought, to Juliana Schwellenberg. Then he turned on his heel and disappeared into the crowd, taking the glow of his presence with him.

Chapter 2

This was not the first – or, he suspected, the last – time Hugh Granville found himself in the bedroom of a woman not his wife. It was very rare indeed, however, for him to do so with the lady in question being absent from the room. Indeed, this was the first time it had happened.

Hugh looked around Lavinia Dudley's bedroom. It was small and tidy – almost too tidy, unnaturally so. It went beyond the efforts of a diligent maid. It looked like a room no one lived in or only a passing guest did – not a woman who, according to his inquiries, had arrived at court three years ago.

The room was located on the ground floor. The logic was clear – the second keeper of the robes had to be close to the queen's apartments in the event of some emergency. The windows looked out onto the bare winter garden. An idyll of dead tranquillity.

Hugh went through the drawers of the desk impatiently. He knew his methods were crass, but it was clear from their exchange at the ball that the talk among male courtiers was true. Each one felt Miss Dudley was a being of icy prudery with an equally icy disapproval of less than perfect behaviour. Had it been otherwise, he would have tried to strike up a friendship with her and pry the news of her latest writings out of her openly – or tease or cajole or flatter them out, if needs be. He knew his cousin Camilla would never leave him alone otherwise once she had learnt her favourite authoress was now moving within Hugh's orbit.

As it were, he was going to resort to less honourable ways to seize the forbidden knowledge. It was not, Hugh told himself, as though he wanted to harm the lady or her work in any way. If good fortune smiled upon him, she would never even know he laid an eye on her latest draft.

Good fortune did smile upon him, and soon enough, he discovered a thin sheath of papers with a title written on top. *Oswald and Elfgiva*.

Interesting. Had she grown tired of the drawing rooms of the ton and decided to throw herself into the distant past? The names alone sounded distinctly Saxon to him. He might have known one Oswald back in Gloucestershire, in the distant green past, but the heroine's name was certainly not the kind found on these isles anymore.

Hugh turned the page carefully and started reading. He was right; the story took place in the murky Dark Ages, in some unspecified time stranded between the conquerors, when monsters roamed the fens. Miss Dudley didn't delve into supernatural horrors, though. The ones she wrote about were very much human made. Siblings feuding, lovers divided, a villain blackmailing the heroine into marriage, and a weak father who talked up a storm about a man's duty, but, when the push came to shove, the father failed to protect the heroine.

It was written in a jagged, tormented torrent of words where only a devotee could have recognised the author of *Miranda*. Nonetheless,

Hugh was somewhat intrigued by how Miss Dudley was going to rescue Elfgiva.

The last chapter showed she didn't. The heroine ended up dead, her white body broken on the black crags.

Hugh had never thought himself to be a person affected by such dark melodrama. There was, however, something unnerving about the contrast between the scream of a story and the neat wintry room it was concealed in.

He set it aside carefully and renewed his search for the unfinished masterpiece he could, write home about. Hugh did find a few unfinished works but not a single masterpiece. They were all variations on the same theme: a setting far enough back in time to be almost mythical, a limp and listless husk of a heroine, an unending torrent of woes, and...walls all around them. He discovered heroines wrongfully imprisoned. Heroines maimed. Heroines forced into marriage. Heroines betrayed by every single higher power they held faith in.

Hugh thought back to the wary, pale face of Miss Dudley. Was all of this a literary exercise, or was there a cauldron of passion and misery boiling behind the impassive courtly mask of a prudent lady?

He found he hoped, perversely, for the latter. Not that he wished her to be miserable – she, unlike some people, had done nothing to him to warrant it. But if she was...he knew just the way to help her.

To help her and to deliver a neat blow to the person who had once slighted him indeed.

This was one of the quiet evening concerts His Majesty delighted in – as some added behind closed doors, in his lucid moments. These people usually preferred the doors in question to be closed very tightly.

The harpsichord always left Lavinia cold, but one could not say so in response to a great honour that was the invitation. If one thought of it, the concerts were almost an institution. Papers, even the more irreverent ones, usually acknowledged it was certainly an improvement on the pastimes of His Majesty's father and a better example than the revels of his son.

When Lavinia saw who was taking his place in the seat by her side, her blood. did not freeze the way it did the night after the ball. Rather, it boiled in irritation. Such a coincidence could only be a mockery by fate. A mockery or a human design.

'I hope tonight brings you pleasure, Miss Dudley,' Lord Granville said after the brief, cold greeting. There was something particularly outrageous in his grin as he said the last three words as though he was promising her pleasures that had nothing to do with a harp or a harpsichord or any other instrument.

A musical instrument, at least.

'I would say I hope so for you, too, your lordship, but I'm afraid my hope is going to be in vain.'

'How right you are, Miss Dudley!' He nodded in mock agreement. 'How right you are! Things here have certainly gone down since Handel's days. I hope Their Majesties still like epic works, though. After all, otherwise they might not enjoy your tragedies.'

Lavinia felt as though the world had grown blurry in front of her eyes, distorting, taking upon itself the outlines of a nightmare.

'My...?' She tried her best to pretend ignorance, but her voice trembled treacherously.

'I know what you have written this summer, Miss Dudley. And this autumn, and likely through Christmas, too.'

'Who dared – who could—' She felt betrayed. Thrown into the mud. A helpless child once more.

'I did. The approaches to your room aren't as well guarded as the approaches to the bedroom of an unwed young woman should be. You give little credit to my daring.'

'You—' The music rose, gentle, crystal bright. Lavinia had to lower her voice, feeling fit to fall through the floor – or strike the man sitting so nonchalantly by her side. 'You cad, you venomous creature—'

'A cad I may be, but I don't see what's so caddish about appreciation for good novels. It is out of my love for them that I want to help you.'

'Help me what, make myself a laughingstock?'

But even as Lavinia spoke these words, a foolish, faint hope stirred in her heart. Perhaps, for all his jeering ways, Lord Granville really was of a mind to help her. He didn't say he disliked her tragedies, after all. Perhaps, he had good connections in the world of arts and letters – perhaps, he even knew Mr Sheridan himself, the proprietor of the Drury Lane Theatre, or—

'No,' Lord Granville replied. 'To escape the court.'

'Why on earth do you think I might want to do such a thing? Queen Charlotte did me a great honour when she offered me the place.'

'I am not a spy for the Crown, Miss Dudley, you don't have to say these rehearsed lines for me. Whatever were your reasons for accepting the offer, it was not a sincere love for the place and not courtly ambition. I've read *Miranda*, and I've read your tragedies—'

'These are nothing,' Lavinia denied hotly. 'Mere scribblations. They weren't meant for prying eyes – for any eyes, really!'

'Scribblations? What a curious word. Did you invent it yourself?' Lord Granville grinned again, this time, curiously, without a touch of wildness or malice. On the contrary, this was the kind of a smile that seemed to bask one's whole face in a sunlit glow and make one seem younger and sweeter in nature.

And Lord Hugh Granville, if one thought about it, didn't even really need this effect. He was, in truth, not older than Lavinia herself, she realised. Somehow, in thinking of him as a seasoned rake, she had mentally added a good decade to his years.

'Let's suppose I did...'

'It's a curious word. Can I write it down?'

'People are looking!'

'Let them think I am an ardent admirer of your talent, writing down the pearls of your prudent words. Although I am not sure if they were to think you just as prudent if they've read *Elfgiva and Her Kin*. It wasn't as bad as some of the tragedies produced on the stage these days, but *Miranda* it was not.'

'Are you a critic now?'

'When I need to be. Would you like to hear my opinion? The plot was as convoluted as a cat's cradle and as bleak as barren rocks.'

'I was drenched in winter misery when I wrote it.'

'The characters might have as well been from a medieval mystery play, what with their virtues and vices.'

'That was deliberate,' Lavinia lied.

'The prose,' Lord Granville said with the air of a man delivering an executioner's blow, 'was terrible. Tortured like prisoners in the Borgia dungeons.'

Lavinia sat speechless. This was indeed a nightmare. Years ago, when she had first published *Miranda* anonymously, before Hester Thrale-Piozzi had taken her under her wing and coaxed her out into the light, these were precisely the kind of words Lavinia feared. To be fair, she feared praise almost as much. She feared any form of fame or recognition that could have allowed people to think her some original high in her instep. But since she was, despite Lord Granville's evident doubts, a human being and not a creature of porcelain, she feared devastation of this kind worst of all.

'Was it truly that bad?' she heard herself asking in a voice not so much soft as small.

'Worse,' Lord Granville replied with an expression of almost gravity. 'Which is why I think you need to escape this place for good. A gifted creature with an airy pen came in, and a living wreck producing literary cries came out? One doesn't need to be a physician to deduce that the place she passed through was probably not the Garden of Eden.'

'Even if I agree...' *Even if I agree that His Majesty's court is to me a soul-crushing place,* Lavinia kept her opinion to herself. Someone might overhear, misunderstand her ironic tone or, indeed, choose to misunderstand and carry the whisper further. Then her career – if not, in this more civilised age, her life – was surely to be under threat. 'Even if we agree that you are right, why would you want to help me? Do I...provoke your interest?'

For a second. it seemed Lord Granville was going to disregard all the rules of decorum that a courtly concert could set and outright laugh. 'Forgive me, Miss Dudley. Truly, forgive me, but you are not the sort of woman who usually provokes my interest. At least, the sort of interest that you are hinting at. For one thing, you are unmarried.'

'What a shameless creature you are, your lordship.'

'On the contrary, I am a very cautious one. The husbands of the ton are a great deal more indifferent than its fathers.'

'Then why?'

'I've already told you. I like good novels and dislike bad tragedies, and this position seems to make you produce less of the former and more of the latter. This cannot stand.'

'Are you going to petition Her Majesty on my behalf?' Lavinia asked, weak hope rearing its head once again.

'I can, but I don't think that would avail me of anything. My standing at court is not exactly exalted.'

'How so? You are His Majesty's equerry!'

'It's a long story. Let us simply say Queen Charlotte has no reasons to feel benevolent towards me.'

He must have seduced one of her ladies-in-waiting, Lavinia decided. Everyone knew what care Her Majesty took of the virtue of the women who attended her.

'No,' Lord Granville continued, 'my plan is a great deal simpler, and, to put it plainly, a great deal merrier. We are going to marry you off.'

'I beg your pardon!'

'Think of it, Miss Dudley. If you are to be Mrs something or other, you would not be able to fulfil your duties as the second keeper of the robes anymore. Her Majesty will have no choice but to allow you to retire to your husband's home.'

'I hope you do realise that, in that case, I would have to live in that home for the rest of my life? A husband is not a new chip hat!'

'No, although there are ladies who take a great more care of the latter than of the former. Do you have a better idea?'

'I do.' She might have been more tempted had the man who offered her this plan was in anyway trustworthy or in any way likely to hold her best interests at heart. But a careless nobleman whose favourite pastime was the seduction of married ladies was most decidedly not either. Lavinia secretly thought every man who violated the sanctity of her writing desk deserved to be hit on the head with a vase. 'We forget about these absurdities and settle down to listen to whatever remains of the concert.'

'Your future is not an absurdity.'

'That is true. I guard it carefully. Forgive me for deeming Her Majesty as better guardian of it than you.'

Lavinia knew she should not have been wasting candles this way. It was, after all, an impossible truth that her being free to retire to bed no earlier than midnight and having to wake up at six in the morning left her little time to sleep, and she might have been wiser using this time to rest. However, if she had little time and less energy to actually write tales of fiction, she could at least carve out a couple of hours to write letters, these remaining her only link with the outside world.

Sometimes, especially when replies took too long, Lavinia wondered if her words ever reached the addressees or if the world beyond St James and Windsor and Kew had drowned in some deadly fog and quietly expired without her noticing. The last time she actually saw anyone from her old life, the life that now seemed half a dream, was months ago, in high summer, when she was walking to the chapel with the others and saw Hester Thrale-Piozzi standing by the palace gate. The memory of that day flooded in.

When Lavinia saw Mrs Thrale-Piozzi standing by the palace gate, she couldn't help but cry out in girlish joy and run to meet the grand dame of the world of letters and her former patroness.

'My, my,' Mrs Thrale-Piozzi said wryly upon looking Lavinia up and down. 'You look so very elegant. Nothing at all like that half-made thing I once received in my house.'

It was a compliment on the face of it; however, Lavinia couldn't help but sense there was something scratching beneath the smooth surface. 'I do miss these dinners in your house, Mrs Thrale-Piozzi.' Lavinia genuinely missed the dinners and wished there could be more.

'You have other duties now, I'm sure.'

'I know you'll understand. You are a married woman again now, after all, and a woman has as many weighty duties to her husband as a servant of the Crown does to her.'

'If you insist so, Miss Dudley. You would know better. I wouldn't say my Signor Piozzi imposes such heavy duties on me.'

'Oh!' Lavinia grasped the offered thread eagerly. 'How were your travels with him? Did he like them? Did you? Did your daughter? And is it true you're planning to write a book about it?'

'A little compendium of letters, more like, after the fashion of Lady Montagu. My real work is my memoirs about Dr Johnson.'

'Will you send me an early copy to read?' Lavinia knew she was crossing all lines with this demand, but it was as if a ravenous maw opened within her and demanded as much as possible while the feeding time still lasted. 'It's only that I have no time to go into town, and no capacity to ask anyone to go for me, and won't be able to find a circulating library or a subscription library or any other kind of library, and—'

Mrs Thrale-Piozzi parted her lips to reply, but Mrs Schwellenberg, who came up to her on the soft courtly slippers, grasped her sleeve and pulled her to the side, none too gently. Lavinia wondered if Mrs Thrale-Piozzi would have delivered a rebuff or a promise if Mrs Schwellenberg hadn't interrupted their conversation.

'Have you lost your wits?' the first keeper of the robes hissed. 'Trying to play truant? Is it faith that you spurn or merely your duty?'

'I am sorry,' Lavinia stammered, the newfound exuberance draining away just as quickly as it came. 'It's only that Mrs Thrale-Piozzi was my good friend.'

If there ever was a woman formidable enough to open her mouth when confronted by a court lady, it was Hester Thrale-Piozzi. She merely raised one eyebrow and asked, 'Was? Miss Dudley, are you angry at me or dead and entombed? Have I been speaking with your ghost as if it were the battlements of Elsinore?'

Mrs Schwellenberg looked her in the eye for the first time instead of scolding Lavinia over her head. Then she leaned closer, and said, 'As far as you are concerned, she might as well be.' She dragged Lavinia away into the slow procession.

Thinking back to that night, Lavinia was less than pleased with her actions – or, rather, her lack of action. It occurred to her now, in the dead of night, there might have been different paths Lavinia could have taken. She could have confronted Mrs Schwellenberg over her outrageous words. She could have torn her hand from her grasp and refused to go.

Or she could have willed herself to become light as air and floated up to the moon. It was about just as likely.

Unfortunately, that had not been the end of the matter. The crowning conclusion of it was more humiliating that anything that preceded it. When the congregation was taking its place in the royal chapel, Queen Charlotte had turned her head and looked straight at Lavinia. She felt frozen to her core now just as she did then. Her

Majesty's words had been sharp when she asked who the painted foreigner was.

Lavinia couldn't remember now what she had invented in response. She only knew it wasn't a dignified refutation of the last descriptor or anything that hinted at Mrs Thrale-Piozzi's reputation, wit, friendship with Dr Johnson, the grand man of letters, or anything else that might have made her deserving of respect.

While the exact words eluded Lavinia now, said as they were in the deadly blaze of the sun that was the royal attention, but it was probably something to the effect of "Forgive me. It was an old friend from my former life."

Lost in these sleepy recollections now, Lavinia did not at first realise the commotion she was hearing in the corridors was not a thing of dreams. She pressed her head against the door as though eavesdropping on the outside world. The twin pair of steps grew closer and then started to recede. Whoever it was, they were walking past her door to some errand of their own.

The wise and prudent thing, Lavinia knew, was to be step aside and leave whoever it was to their business. For all she knew, it could be a pair of illicit lovers. For all she knew, it could be Lord Granville with his paramour of the month, his arm draped around her waist, his hand probably hanging loose, and his fingers touching the lady's behind or stroking her waist with languorous movements. If so, the woman's face was most likely flushed bright with pleasure and the anticipation of more of it. That could account for the hurry in the footsteps…

Lavinia opened the door and stepped out into the corridor. If he, or any other rake, wanted to carry his liaison out, it was not going to happen outside her door.

Caustic remarks that could have belonged on a page were already forming in her thoughts, and then she saw something that stopped her in her tracks. These were not lovers. The pair were two ladies-in-waiting, one almost Lavinia's age, one significantly older, and writ on their faces was pure panic.

'What happened?' Lavinia asked breathlessly.

The older one didn't even dignify her with a turn of the head. The younger one paused in her frenetic walking – no woman of breeding and no woman who served as a lady-in-waiting would ever do something as uncouth as break into a run – and said breathlessly, 'Her Majesty screamed.'

Blood drained from Lavinia's face. All the horrific tales of French émigrés she ever heard before coming to court flared up in her memory and populated her mind with thoughts of assassinations and revolutionaries. She didn't pause to put on her shoes or think. She hurried down the corridor.

It took them a long time to reach the royal bedchamber. It took so long that Lavinia wondered, briefly, fearfully, just how loud the scream must have been for it to reach the women she was now following – and what could have caused it.

When the door to the sacred space finally opened, Lavinia saw a strange, chiaroscuro picture: a darkened opulence, several candles burning by the bed, a pale woman upon it – and an old man leaning over her.

Lavinia didn't think this time either. She simply grabbed one of the candelabras standing by the bed and raised it high. The younger lady-in-waiting squealed and caught her hand before Lavinia could bring the heavy object down on the villain's head. Astonished by this betrayal, Lavinia turned to her, ready for a struggle, when the older lady cried out.

'Your Majesty! We are terribly sorry – we thought your wife is...u nwell!'

Your wife? Lavinia stared at the man crouching by the royal bed. He seemed to have very little in common with the father of the nation, the rose-cheeked farmer king whom every loyal subject born within the last few decades was taught – not always successfully – to love. But the more she looked, the more she recognised the features she glimpsed during the few – within the last few years, very few indeed – public royal appearances.

She had just almost hit the King George on the head with a candelabra. Perhaps, Mrs Schwellenberg had a point when she thought Lavinia didn't belong at court.

'So, you know of her illness, too?' King George asked, not letting go of his silent wife's hand.

There was no way to tell a man with a crown, however afflicted his mind, that you had no idea what he was talking about. Therefore, the trio remained silent, blinking politely.

'My dear Charlotte has a cold.' There was impatience in his voice but no anger. 'Where on earth are her physicians? Some of them are such untrustworthy men. You cannot expect them to care about their patient a whit. Don't you agree, Amelia?'

The last words were addressed, shockingly, to Lavinia. He was taking her for Princess Amelia, his beloved little daughter. His daughter might have been as beautiful and sweet-natured as a princess ought to be, but she was not yet ten years old, much younger than Lavinia.

What was Lavinia to do? What could anyone, much less a person with a crumb of compassion in them, do but play along?

'I do,' she said, avoiding calling him father. It might have helped to placate him, but who knew what rumour the very much sane ladies in the room might make of it in the future. 'They are slippery. Slippery as eels.'

'What a good girl you are, Amelia. And how you've grown! You will be a good companion to your mother. Your future husband will be a happy man.' A kind of tenderness touched King George's expression.

'I doubt she is going to marry,' Queen Charlotte ventured, clearly adept in the art of sustaining illusions. 'I need Amelia here, just as I need her sisters. I hope you don't want me to remain lonely as they marry away?'

'Of course not, dear Charlotte. Besides, marriages of blood are so seldom as happy as ours. Do you remember what happened to poor Mathilde when father sent her away?'

It was as though Queen Charlotte's body turned to stone. Her features went set, her arms rigid, and her voice strict as that of a schoolmistress as she said, 'We do not talk about that woman in the presence of our daughters. Illness or no illness.'

'Your Majesty,' the older lady-in-waiting ventured, 'how did you hear of Her Majesty's...indisposition?'

'Why, I didn't need to hear of it! I always know when my wife is unwell. She knows all about my complaints, too, or else she wouldn't have surrounded me with so many doctors.' His smile was one of true tenderness, but his eyes glinted just as strangely. 'Luckily, I know how to escape their attentions when they become unbearable. We all need our little tricks. Don't we, Charlotte?'

At the mention of regular escapes, the queen's face grew paler than before. She barely resembled the lady who once publicly scolded Lavinia in the chapel – the lady of splendid, voluminous robes, perfect poise and glittering attendants. The woman lying in front of her now was white-faced, shadow-eyed, and, despite the presence in the room of three people besides her husband, incredibly, utterly alone.

The younger lady-in-waiting made use of everyone's attention being directed away from her and started sidestepping quietly towards the door. She didn't get very far.

King George turned sharply, facing her, and this time, anger was writ darkly upon his features. 'What sort of an attendant are you, young lady, if you want to abandon your queen in an hour of need? Is it for this that your parents sent you to court? Great honours come with responsibilities!'

'I – I know, Your Majesty,' the young woman stammered.

'Then don't forget it. Come here. Sit. You are a lady-in-waiting, aren't you?'

'Yes, Your Majesty.'

'So wait. Your queen might have a need of you before the dawn comes.'

'I assure you, you don't need to worry.' The perfectly healthy Queen Charlotte intervened. 'I feel…I feel much better.'

'It's better to be sure. Fevers are a horrid thing. Amelia, come closer. Your mother needs your company and good cheer.'

My mother is dead, Lavinia thought as she knelt by the royal bed. Her knees soon started to hurt even despite the costly rug that separated her from the hard floors. Through her closed eyelids, she could see the flares that were the lonely candles, amber in the darkness.

The night beyond the windows was at full height, and Lavinia knew it was going to be long, long hours before the moon was going to begin its descent and cede its place to the sun.

Chapter 3

Lavinia was walking through the garden paths with frenetic, nervous energy, born of a mixture of urgency and fear. What if she miscalculated? What if the royal equerries did not rise so early or did not take walks here, or if they did rise early to take walks, what if the man she was seeking did not? What if Mrs Schwellenberg was to look for her and find her dutiful little room empty? What if—

She let out a breath when she saw the group of strapping young men walking among the spring greenery. They were a picture of masculine good cheer, talking about something animatedly between themselves. They could as well have walked out of another world, so far was their mood from Lavinia's dark turmoil.

In other circumstances, she would have felt too fearful to approach them; after all, she had only been actually introduced to one of them. And even so, she could not simply intrude and drag him away from his fellows. But here and now, her thoughts and decisions were ruled by a different rationale. In some cases, she reasoned, good manners could perhaps be sacrificed to expediency – if the situation was dire enough, of course. As far as she was concerned, the situation was dire enough.

'Your lordship,' she addressed Lord Granville, who was at the forefront of the group. 'Would you mind if we speak?'

'Lavinia Dudley agreeing to talk to someone like me without a chaperone? Hell must have frozen over.'

'It's rather urgent,' she pleaded. 'We are not going to walk far – your friends would see us all the time – no one would suspect an intrigue or—'

'Miss Dudley, I was only teasing you.' Hugh Granville's green gaze softened a little. 'Teasing you, in fact, seems a delicious pastime of late. Of course, we can walk.'

Lavinia gave him a grateful smile. As she took his offered arm, she tried her best to ignore the surprised and interested glances of the male courtiers. The glances were understandable – if this did not smell of intrigue, it smelled of flirtation. They also felt like a white-hot iron to the back of her head.

'Is your offer still in force?' she whispered when they took only a few steps away.

'My offer to marry you?' he said. 'To someone else, that is?' he added with a twinkle in his eye.

'Your offer to help me escape.'

'Well, the trip to Cheltenham hasn't come and gone, has it? That means we still have plenty of time. But' – he raised a finger, pre-empting her reply – 'I would first like to know what caused such a change of opinion.'

'Perhaps, I came to my senses and realised what a splendid source of guidance you are.'

'You would have to try better than that if you want to convince me, Miss Dudley.'

'What do you care?' she all but snapped and flushed when she realised her slip.

Lord Granville looked at her with new eyes, but thankfully, the look in them was surprised, not offended.

'Miss Dudley.' He softened his voice below any register demanded by secrecy. 'What exactly has happened?'

'Nothing. His Majesty...' It was easy for pamphlet writers and Grub Street hacks, living as they did far from here, to gleefully write *His Majesty is stark raving mad*. Lavinia, who existed now close to the unbearably shining centre of power, couldn't even force herself to utter the words *made a mistake*. 'His Majesty thought Her Majesty was sick. He came to her in the night, and I happened to be there, and...'

'Ah, so the old Farmer George is raving again?'

'Your lordship!'

'Your reprimands would have sounded less feeble if you weren't as white as a sheet.'

'I was only – a little shaken...'

'So little shaken that you even neglected your duties today to run and find me.'

'I didn't neglect anything. I have no duties today. They... Her Majesty has decided it might be better' – she didn't say safer – 'to humour His Majesty's fantasy and stayed in bed for the day. My services of dressing her are not required.'

'I see.' He said those two words with something that almost approached sincerity. He raised his left hand, and for a second, Lavinia thought he was going to squeeze her fingers in an attempt to soothe her. She froze at the thought of all those men watching them, men who had ears and mouths and wagging tongues, no less than women did, whatever some claimed.

Fortunately, Lord Granville evidently thought better of it, and he allowed his hand to drop back. Lavinia was relieved, of course, that he didn't give fodder to rumours, but deep down – she must have been distraught indeed – she was just a little disappointed she had not experienced the touch of his gloved hand against hers. He did, she noticed, have rather elegant fingers.

'Is there anyone in particular you thought I could...ask to take me away?' Her gaze slid involuntarily over to the group of his friends.

'Not as you are now.'

'Whatever do you mean?'

'The sorts of men you are looking at, the sorts of men who can insist upon marriage and risk Her Majesty's displeasure, need dowries, not manuscripts. It's not that they never marry ravishing beauties with only a few pounds a year to their name, but...'

'...but I am not a ravishing beauty,' Lavinia finished for him. This sort of frankness had drained out of her like blood in the hands of a medieval physician soon after she had arrived at court, but something in Lord Granville's manner made confessions easy.

That fact made her wonder if her portrait of the villainous seducer in *Miranda* was all wrong. Perhaps, most of such men weren't sleek, dark, and dangerous; perhaps, they rather had a gift to elicit laughter and anger alike from their would-be conquests at the drop of a hat, and they later turned these to more heated sensations.

'Perhaps, not, but you can be made to resemble one very well.'

'How?'

'With a bit of money and the right clothes. I can provide the former, and I'm sure you know a mantua maker who will supply the latter. If anyone asks, you want to be well turned out for the royal visit.'

'What are people going to think if they see you paying my bills?'

'My dear Miss Dudley, do you really think I haven't yet learnt to pay a woman's bills in a way that doesn't allow anyone to see it?'

'Why are you doing this for me?' Lavinia asked bluntly, unnerved. She was not a fool enough to think that unprompted and honest generosity, especially as flowing from young men to young women they were not married to, existed in this world.

'I've told you that already.'

'Yes, you like good novels and hate bad tragedies.'

'Ah, so you remembered my words verbatim! I am flattered.'

'You don't have to be, Lord Granville, for I didn't believe them. That is, I readily believe you like good novels, but I don't think it's enough of a reason for you to try to circumvent the royal will.'

'What if I told you, Miss Dudley, that circumventing the royal will is the whole purpose?'

Lavinia frowned. Surely, he was joking. There was no way a young equerry would want to deceive Queen Charlotte deliberately, unless for some great gain. Unless... 'Are you doing this for a lark?'

For a second, his lips pressed together in a way that, perplexingly, spoke of frustration, even anger. Then the skies cleared, and Lord Hugh Granville became his sunlit self again.

'Yes, Miss Dudley. For a lark. Are you going to assist me in this lark?'

Lavinia reflected on her choices and realised she had very few of them.

'Yes, your lordship,' she said. 'I will.'

'God Almighty,' the mantua maker said upon entering Lavinia's room. 'One would have thought that with all the gilt and finery they have in this place, and all the space and light, they would have found you a better place to sleep in than this.'

'I am perfectly satisfied with my accommodation, Mrs Hunt,' Lavinia said dutifully, the words like well-worn smooth pebbles in her mouth. Her inner voice murmured to her that she would run no risk by complaining about it to a complete outsider, a woman who had no connection to court and thus was unlikely to wag her tongue about it with anyone who mattered here. But the key to self-restraint was an iron habit, and to break it even once could have meant making the whole construction crash down one day.

'If you say so, my dear. I can imagine your room at home was somewhat bigger, though.' Mrs Hunt, who used to dress Lavinia's late mother before she began dressing Lavinia, had never precisely seen the inside of the Dudleys' household – they were not of such rank as to be visited by a mantua maker in the comfort of their home. Her guess, however, was quite correct.

Lavinia replied with a noncommittal noise of the sort that could be interpreted equally as an assent, a negation, and an expression of indifference to the whole matter.

'I suppose your new position has consolations,' Mrs Hunt continued. 'All those young bucks at court! It is for them that you are now looking to dress yourself up a little, isn't it?'

'Mrs Hunt.' Lavinia blushed. 'I have no such intention. It is only that I have realised I hadn't anything new in my wardrobe, and...'

'You don't need to fib to me, Miss Dudley. Nothing sinful about wanting to get married well. That is why you've come to court, haven't you?'

Lavinia was startled. Was that what they were saying about her? That her reason for accepting the queen's offer was not to honour her family, advance her father's career and her own, but to claw her way up into the ton?

She couldn't well deny that charge all that vehemently, though. Not now. Not anymore. Instead, she decided to respond with a secretive smile.

'I knew you were a sensible girl.' Mrs Hunt nodded. 'Do you have any ideas of what you want?'

'I think...a half dress, maybe? Of...' Lavinia paused, then forced herself to recall money was no objection for a while. 'Of satin. Grey.'

'Satin? But it's long since past time you had a proper spring suit! Only a demi-saison silk will do for one of those.'

'That's...' Lavinia's first urge was to say too expensive. 'Reasonable.'

'Grey is not your colour either. Well, it is if you want to impress the gentlemen with your becoming modesty, but in my experience, they are only impressed by it on the pages of conduct books. They might seek this quality in a wife, but to entice them down the aisle, it would not do.'

'I do hope you aren't saying I must don something crimson?' Lavinia teased her old acquaintance.

'Of course not. Crimson is not your colour. Pale blue would do much better. Sleeves white crepe, edged with blond. I think the Bertin colours would all fit you well.'

'The Bertin colours?'

'The hues she used to dress the poor late French queen in. Powder blue, soft yellow, some green... The fabrics might be too daring for these shores – I've heard Her Majesty has strict views on female attire – but the colours would do very well.'

The poor late French queen. Lavinia had heard these words very often the last – how long was it? Six months, seven? People spoke sombrely of the death of monarchs and the end of a great era of French predominance, but there was also a suppressed relief in their words: 'Thank God it did not happen here; thank God our Queen Charlotte is alive and well.' And, deep down, people were grateful Queen Charlotte was a paragon of virtue. No Grub Street hack would dare to imply she was having an affair, and no demagogue would find words to turn mobs against her. The people were thankful Her Majesty was a pillar of propriety, the shining star of all becoming womanly qualities.

'There is an idea I had for a while,' Mrs Hunt continued, 'but I wasn't sure what to do with it. Most women I dress, they, to be frank, do not have the means for something of the kind – and you, I thought, would not have the desire. But now that that has changed...'

She did not search for the drawing all that long, Lavinia noticed. That meant she didn't have it buried as deep as she implied. If anything, she must have prepared it before she came here. After all, who would have both the money and the wish for whatever magnificent creation Mrs Hunt's imagination produced, if not the prodigy of the Dudleys, who was doubtless thriving at court?

Lavinia looked at the drawing in question, and the vision filled her with sudden yearning. The creation-to-be was a dress of pale-green silk with a tiffany petticoat, festooned with lilacs. On her head, the faintly sketched figure wore a headdress of white feathers.

'The headdress is not for every day, of course,' Mrs Hunt clarified as though that needed clarification. 'Only for the 'queen's drawing room days, perhaps.'

Yes, Lavinia reflected, it would do for the drawing rooms very well, just as the gown itself would do very well for less formal evening occasions.

If I can afford it. The thought entered her head, unbidden, propelled by the sheer force of habit. She could afford it now, technically, but a lifetime of thrift could not be overcome by a single promise to pay for one extravagance.

Perhaps not just one. If Lord Granville really was serious about what he called his lark – a paradox in words in itself, perhaps something that she would do well to remember for a future piece of writing – he might pay for all the extravagances the occasion demanded. Most likely, he was as generous, if not more so, with the ladies he graced with his attentions in a different way.

The thought filled her with distaste, no doubt stemming from her lack of acquaintance with that side of ton life. Lavinia swallowed, trying to banish the bile that rose to her throat for a second. The humorous imaginings of showering Lord Granville's desk with unpaid bills disappeared from her mind.

'I am sorry,' Lavinia said. 'I...I don't think I could wear something of this kind,'

'Whyever not?'

'I... It's too short.' She found a flaw to focus on. 'See, it almost bares my ankles!'

'Oh, dear child, but you have such pretty ankles! If you were to find graceful enough slippers, you would look an angel. Well, not an angel. Men, be they nobility or petty traders or paupers for that matter, would take a woman of flesh and blood over a floating angel anytime.'

'When you say take, do you mean...'

'To wife, of course,' Mrs Hunt replied, a picture of innocence. 'What else? Unless the floating angel has a large dowry.'

'You have always been a very pragmatic woman.'

'I have, yes. I am proud of the fact. Your mother was no dreaming seraph, either – I've known her. If she were still alive, perhaps you wouldn't have bricked yourself up in that high tower of sermon ideas. Too short indeed! You are trying to catch a husband, dear Lavinia, not impress some Spanish monk.'

To catch a husband. Her aim could easily be distilled in those four words. Yes, Lavinia Dudley – the woman who had prided herself on living the life of the mind and daughterly duty – was indeed out to catch a husband so that she could evade that duty. And, in order to do so, she was accepting financial gifts from a rakish gentleman whose aims were known only to himself.

Sermon ideas indeed. Perhaps, all that she was looking for was per-mission to rebel, and the night of terror in the company of a mad king and a frightened queen gave her exactly that.

The rebellion would be short-lived, Lavinia promised herself. It was not likely to last the year. Or, should she be so fortunate, a month.

'Perhaps, you are right,' she said, lowering her gaze in what felt like a parody of her usual withdrawing ways. 'Perhaps, I do need this gown with a tiffany petticoat.'

It was seven in the morning, and Lavinia, who had to rise at six, was not in a mood for surprises. Nonetheless, surprise was what she felt when she hurried down the corridor leading from her room in the 'queen's apartments and almost ran into Mrs Schwellenberg.

'Good morning,' Lavinia said, pressing down the sense of unease rising in her heart. She knew the first keeper of the robes never rose so early in the morning. The process of dressing Queen Charlotte's hair and person was begun by the soft-spoken German Mrs Thielky and finished by Lavinia herself. Mrs Thielky dealt with her coiffure, and Lavinia assisted with her clothing, passing the hoop and gown, slippers, neck handkerchief and finally the fan to Mrs Thielky who passed each item to Her Majesty.. Mrs Schwellenberg came in nowhere in this process; she was, if anything, something more of an honourable companion than a quiet servant of the kind Lavinia herself now was.

'I do wish I could have said the same, Miss Dudley,' the first keeper of the robes replied, her iron-grey eyes implacable. 'I have been seeking you many an afternoon, but it seems you are very busy. With a mantua maker, of all people.'

'I apologize.' Lavinia could not keep a certain irritated haste out of her voice. She had a duty to perform, and she could not imagine the consequences if she were too late for the dressing ceremony. Or, rather, for the ceremony of passing clothing items to Mrs Thielky so that she could perform the dressing proper.

'Do you think me simple, Miss Dudley?'

'I beg your pardon?'

'You have affected the modesty of a church mouse, all these years you have been my charge here.'

Lavinia winced internally at the wording. Her charge indeed – as though she were a perpetual schoolgirl and Mrs Schwellenberg her governess who was never to be sent away.

'Yet now,' the older woman continued, 'you are suddenly decking yourself out in finery. I have happened to overhear some of your conversations with that Mrs Hunt. Silk! Satin! One might have thought you were deeming yourself a noble heiress!'

I had no idea, Lavinia thought archly, *that the medieval sumptuary laws were still enforced in our country and only noble heiresses could legally wear certain good fabrics.* She shut the thought down almost before it fully formed. Rationally, she knew no one at court could read her mind. Irrationally, she had taught herself to be careful, just in case. After all, a person unguarded in their thoughts was likely to be unguarded in their words one day, too.

'I assure you, Mrs Schwellenberg, I had no such notions.'

'I have always thought you a woman with unseemly desires. Desires to rise above your station, of course. Else you would not have had the brazen cheek to accept this post when Her Majesty offered it out of graciousness.'

'Do you think it would have been any less brazen of me to deny the honour Her Majesty decided to give me?'

'In that case, yes,' Mrs Schwellenberg said bluntly. 'But your behaviour does not stop there, does it? Do you think I do not know where pretty young women with no lineage suddenly get the money to spend on silk and satin where previously a lawn hood was out of the realm of possibility?'

'Mrs Schwellenberg, I have no idea,' Lavinia lied. She had every idea, in fact, and wanted the ground to swallow her whole.

'They find themselves protectors,' Mrs Schwellenberg replied with utter disdain. 'Obliging gentlemen who pay their bills in return for discreet favours in dark corners.'

'I assure you it's not true in my case.' Three years ago, before she came to court, even two years ago, before it grew into her bones, Lavinia would have erupted in response to such an insinuation. Now, like a giddy chit tamed into a good wife, she knew better.

'Her Majesty is going to hear of it, if it is true indeed,' the first keeper of the robes threatened. 'And then, Miss Dudley, you are going to rue the day you decided to ape your betters and insert yourself into their ranks.'

'You should not worry, Mrs Schwellenberg,' Lavinia replied with becoming meekness, allowing herself to finish the phrase in her mind.

For Her Majesty is not going to hear about the source of this largesse. 'The money comes from the success of my father's latest work. The third tome of his history of German music is now on sale in Mr Wickman's printing shop.'

'I had no idea music is such a profitable business in this country. Though, I suppose, I should have guessed as much. Were it not, music teachers would have never been able to see their daughters serve at court.' With this parting shot, the first keeper of the robes stepped aside, and allowed Lavinia to pass.

The courtyard of Windsor Castle, usually orderly, was in pandemonium today on the eve of the court's departure to Cheltenham. The air was sharp with the tang of horses, which was unnaturally sweetened with hundreds of competing perfumes. Those who recalled the original visit to Cheltenham in '88 claimed the departure was an even more chaotic affair back then. It was, after all, before the new fashions from the Continent did away with panniers and powdered wigs, and fitting all that into a carriage was pure Herculean labour.

Lavinia herself wore her hair natural, albeit more out of convenience than modishness. So did plenty of younger court ladies for one reason or another. Few were bold enough to wear the French-style flowing gowns that left so little to the imagination in the presence of Queen Charlotte and her virtuous companions of Mrs Schwellenberg's ilk. Lavinia regretted that. Had they indeed worn those dresses with their simple Grecian outlines, the business of arranging everyone in the vehicles would have gone much easier.

'We can put some of the trunks inside my carriage,' Mrs Schwellnberg insisted to one of the footmen.

'But then you would barely have any room for your own person, not to mention you companion's.'

'Miss Dudley would manage, I imagine. So will I, if needs must.'

Lavinia gulped as she imagined exactly how she was going to manage in a cramped space over the many hours of the journey in proximity to the woman who loathed her and anything that could give her comfort. The order of the words in the Mrs Schwellenberg's statement was not lost on her. Words were, after all, her tools of trade.

She turned away, ardently looking for any vehicle that seemed to be at least half full, even if it didn't belong to anyone she knew. She knew how horrible it would be of her to impose so on anyone else, but it was less horrible than the notion of a whole day in a closet's worth of space with the first keeper of the robes.

When she saw Lord Granville on the step to his carriage emblazoned with a bright crest, she almost cried out for joy. She bit her lip, of course, forcing the display of emotion down. However, something must have reflected in her stare, for, when their eyes met, Lord Granville paused.

He stepped down and strode over to her. It was no easy task, for, despite the courtyard being filled with great ladies and the pinks of fashion, they jostled no less than a crowd at a fish market and were affronted a great deal easier. He did not barge through them as much as he glided – a charming smile there, a quick mollifying apology there – and the glittering throng parted for him as though he were a prophet and they the waters of the Red Sea.

'Miss Dudley,' Lord Granville said. 'What a pleasant surprise. How may I be of service?' His question, usually a mere tribute to politesse, sounded urgent.

God Almighty, I must look terrified. Lavinia attempted to compose herself more fully. 'There is a trouble with Mrs Schwellenberg's luggage. We might not fit into the carriage. Or...'

'Or you might, but it's going to be an utterly hellish situation if you do?' he said. 'Good thing my own carriage is gaping with emptiness. I would be honoured if you shared the journey with me.'

Everything in Lavinia, every nerve in her body, screamed out to say yes. This yearning had nothing to do with 'his lordship's easy charm, quick wit, or the way the spring sun turned his fair hair into gold. She was too sensible for such notions. No – she had a much better reason: namely, the refuge he was going to give her.

But then, he had no sister, no living mother, no female relative travelling with him. What if someone thought they did something untoward during the long journey to Cheltenham?

It was this lingering doubt, this fatal delay, that cost Lavinia the hours of a tête-à-tête with Lord Hugh Granville. For, while she was prevaricating, Mrs Schwellenberg, whose hearing had always been as sharp as her manners were proper, had time to react.

'Absolutely not,' she replied flatly. 'Forgive me, your lordship, I am casting no aspersions on your reputation, but people might imagine all kinds of things at their dish of scandal broth.' She said it without much effort to disguise the fact she very much was trying to cast aspersions on his reputation.

'Perhaps, then, you yourself could take her place in my carriage. Even if it is the den of iniquity on wheels as you suppose, such a well-reputed matron as you would never cause rumours.'

For a second – a second only – Lavinia envied Lord Granville the ease and mockery with which he spoke his opinion. For a second – a second only – she yearned for it as a crippled child might yearn for the flight of a bird. That yearning lasted only a second.

'Where, then, will Miss Dudley go?'

'I would have thought that obvious. Miss Dudley would travel in your carriage. There should be enough room for one, especially if the one in question is such a slight young woman.'

'Miss Dudley? In my carriage?' Mrs Schwellenberg asked acidly. 'Why, your lordship, I am surprised you haven't proposed I give my gloves up to her, too, and my post in the bargain!'

'Come, Mrs Schwellenberg. Everyone knows you for a woman of Spartan stoicism, but would you truly prefer discomfort when offered its opposite?'

The first keeper of the robes looked at him and then at Lavinia. Turning her head slightly, she looked at the trunks being loaded, even now, into her carriage. 'We accept your gracious offer, Lord Granville, but on one condition only. Miss Dudley's virtue is in my charge, and I am going to travel with you to ensure nothing threatens it.'

'Would you? I thought you said the only threat to her virtue are the gossips who are going to discuss this arrangement over their dishes of tea, not anything that I myself can do.' His sunny face was innocence itself. 'But, of course, far be it for me to disappoint a lady.'

He left it hanging in the air, never clarifying which of the two women – the older or the younger, the venerable or the interloper – did he just dignify with the title of a lady.

Chapter 4

L ord Granville was not sure what on earth possessed him to offer the keepers of the robes his carriage for the duration of the travels. He might have hoped that the presence of ladies, especially one with whom he was now bound by a most delicious conspiracy, would enliven the journey. If so, he was to be sorely disappointed – Mrs Schwellenberg, this bastion of old-fashioned pannier skirts, was looking at him disapprovingly, and Miss Dudley kept an uncharacteristic silence.

The older lady, Hugh noticed, was certainly not new to the chains of commanding. As soon as they settled in their seats, she put the glass separating the carriage from the open air down. Hugh couldn't account for her desire; the day was cold for spring and still filled with the bracing chill of the night's rain. He didn't find the result altogether agreeable, but he said nothing. Poking fun at such battle-axes was one thing. Starting a brawl with a lady within the confines of one's vehicle at the beginning of a long journey was another.

His gaze fell on Lavinia Dudley. There was a sensible shawl around her shoulders, but her hands, usually resting upon her knees, were now clutching it, pulling it tighter around herself. As a result, Hugh couldn't help but notice her shoulders were rather high and shapely. He also couldn't help but notice her eyes were rather reddish as was her nose.

'Mrs Schwellenberg,' the authoress said, and Hugh was amazed by how tremulous her voice sounded. 'Would you mind putting the glass up again, please?'

'Why?' the older lady asked archly. 'Does fresh air displease you?'

'No, of course not, it is only that I – might have a mild cold.' She sounded.. embarrassed by the fact as though she might have contracted it on purpose.

'A mild cold,' Mrs Schwellenberg repeated. 'How very convenient. Do such illnesses always assail you at the prospect of any discomfort?'

If there was anything Hugh disliked in life – no, in fact, he disliked rather a lot of things – but plain unreason was always at the top of the list. 'I am no physician,' he said, 'but it's evident even to my own eyes that Miss Dudley is unwell.'

'Madame Haggerdorn used to travel with me in winter in this manner,' she replied briskly. 'And she was a great deal older than Miss Dudley here but complained very rarely at all. She had a maid make a concoction of milk and butter for her eyes afterwards and did her duty.'

'Miss Dudley's duty is to Her Majesty. Not...' He was sorely tempted to say not to some jumped-up harpy. But Hugh held his tongue. 'Not to you, Mrs Schwellenberg, with all due respect. Miss Dudley, do put the glass up.'

Lavinia Dudley obeyed him with the same silent efficiency with which she obeyed the first keeper of the robes in the first place, and the sight of it enraged Hugh more than any hauteur in Mrs Schwellenberg's speech, any unreason in her ways, could have done.

At the sight of this rebellion, the older woman nearly gasped. 'What manner is this, Miss Dudley? Put the glass down at once! I will not have this behaviour from a woman of your kind. You will bear the air just fine. It's not as though it was January outside!.

Hugh had had enough. He leaned a little forward – not close enough to be an open intruder but close enough for the older lady to feel a kind of a threat – and said, as mildly as possible, 'You will have this behaviour, Mrs Schwellenberg. Indeed, you will have any behaviour Miss Dudley would see fit to exhibit even if she decides to dance on the roof of this vehicle. Because this is my carriage. You probably think that I offered you a place in it out of deference to your exalted position and years. You are mistaken. I offered it to you because the idea amused me. If your tantrums will amuse me no longer, I am going to offer this place to another.'

Blood drained from Mrs Schwellenberg's face. Miss Dudley was watching in numb, horrified fascination as though an earthquake or the eruption of Vesuvius was unfolding in front of her very eyes.

'But, Lord Granville...you cannot be implying you will simply – exile me into another's care like a misbehaving schoolgirl!'

'I very much can. Moreover, you will have to find another who will take you into his care yourself because I am an impatient man and new to the ways of the court. I don't have many friends here to whom I could offer such an ordeal as your company without breaking the bonds of friendship forever. But the royal train is long, and I am sure you will find some kind soul among its carriages.'

Mrs Schwellenberg's lips parted as though she was a fish gasping in dry air. Up close, the look was comical.

'Keep the glass up, Miss Dudley,' Hugh added in a pleasant voice, leaning back. 'If this be a rebellion, I am giving you a permission to rebel.'

The most famous theatre in Cheltenham – of the two that existed in the town, at any rate – was a beautiful construction. It was smaller than those London theatres Lavinia once visited with her father years ago, in another life, but it was exquisitely decorated, and the velvet that decorated the boxes was freshly cut and deeply crimson.

In another time, Lavinia would have greatly enjoyed the performance. It had been an eternity since she had been out on the town this way, enjoying great stories and observing other people who enjoyed them without any hurry. As it was, three things worried at her, preventing the enjoyment in question.

One, they had only arrived in Cheltenham hours before and barely had time to freshen their appearances, let alone rest or eat. The grateful and patriotic citizens, however, expected Their Majesties to make an appearance in the royal box, and it would not have done to start the royal trip with disappointing grateful and patriotic citizens.

Two, Lavinia was still shaken by the incident in the carriage. She knew she was going to pay for it in some other way, most likely by enduring a thousand more snipes and pinches than usual. Lavinia believed it a truth universally known that a person who cannot punish the exalted personage who snubbed them was going to look for a more vulnerable victim closer to home. But still, it had been startling to see Lord Granville to come to her defence. To see anyone at this court come to her defence. Lavinia had grown accustomed to a dutiful invisibility she had never really had to endure in her father's house.

Three, tonight was supposed to be the first step in her – her and Lord Granville's – plan. The first time she was to put her fine attire into use.

'It's a marvellous performance, isn't it?' Lavinia ventured in a whisper, addressing one of the older equerries who accompanied them in their box. He was a widower, which Lavinia had ascertained through quiet inquiries before they left for Cheltenham. She was nothing if not thorough and had resolved to stick to smooth and empty pleasantries to improve her odds.

Instead of the widower replying, Kurt von Wallmoden replied, 'It is. Though it would have been more marvellous still if they had put on *A School for Scandal* as they had initially planned instead of substituting it for the weakest version of *King Lear* known to man. I imagine the company feared to offend my esteemed relative's sensibilities.'

The relative part was stretching it, and Lavinia knew it. Kurt von Wallmoden was technically the grandson of the second George, but his father had been born of a liaison outside that late monarch's eventful marriage. It was a great clemency on the present king's part, she thought, to call the younger child of that unfortunate line from the small German court he usually resided in and give him a place among the splendour of St James and Windsor. Not that the dark-haired buck looked particularly grateful just at the moment.

'The weakest version of *King Lear*?' Lavinia asked, widening her eyes for effect, as though she had never heard about the famous rewrite that gave the Bard's tragedy a happy ending.

Men, she had heard plenty of times, did not like being contradicted, much less corrected. She had never given the statement much thought before, for marriage was never in her plans. She had made herself useful as her father's amanuensis and later earned a good living by her pen, and in neither of those situations did she want to leave the comforts of maidenhood. Now, however, she did not have a choice. It was transformation or prison. Therefore, she widened her eyes and leaned in to hear better.

'This version, the one where the virtuous daughter triumphs with an army and marries the no less virtuous hero, is a "correction" made merely decades ago,' he explained. 'In the original, she dies in her father's arms.'

'How very horrible,' Lavinia somehow managed to say with a straight face. As if she, who had once been a great reader, could have conceivably never known of it. As if she, whose purpose in life was to craft stories, was the kind of person to think ancient tragedies horrible instead of cleansing.

'Do not worry, Miss Dudley. As you can see, the play has been updated for our more civilised age, and the good heroine is going to get her due.'

'It's always a joy, isn't it, when virtue is rewarded?'

'That depends on what the virtue in question is. Some claim weakness and inaction is a virtue. For a lady, that may be true, but I cannot imagine a man living by this pious claim and still holding any regard for himself.'

Then why on earth are you not out there fighting the French? Lavinia thought. But, of course, she could not say so. 'I imagine your royal kinsman has all the regard in the world, and he is said to be the mildest of men.'

'That he certainly is,' Kurt von Wallmoden agreed. 'However, I would not have wanted to live my life to say that I have only read of daring deeds in books. I understand it's different for you, Miss Dudley, you being a lady.'

Mrs Schwellenberg, who was sitting to Lavinia's left hand, was not having the best of days or weeks, that much was plain. Lavinia noticed her sharp little glance at the last remark. It was not difficult to decipher; the 'king's own relative, if a distant one and with a parent born on the wrong side of the blanket, had just paid Lavinia a grand compliment.

He had not called her a woman. He had called her a lady. Lavinia resisted the temptation to glance at the back of the box where Lord Granville was currently sitting and no doubt enjoying the play immensely. Both plays.

'It is different, yes,' Lavinia agreed meekly, showing her gratitude with a nod.

'I happen to know Cheltenham has good circulating libraries. It pays host to the best society after Bath and London, after all, and caters to all sorts of needs.'

'Such as?' The eagerness tore through her tone however much Lavinia tried to conceal it.

'There is Mr Harward's library by the Colonnade.'

Lavinia dropped her fan. She bent down for it, quicker than thought, unladylike, transported for a second into her earlier life where there were no solicitous gentlemen to pick up the scarves and the shawls and the fans she happened to clumsily drop.

But, if she was quicker than thought, Kurt von Wallmoden was quicker than her. His fingers closed around the handle first, and he whispered, barely audible, 'We could meet there at three in the afternoon tomorrow. I do like their selection.'

Lavinia only had a split second to reply. To decide how to reply. This was improbable. Impossible. Noblemen of his rank, even foreign ones, even the sons of royal bastards, did not fall for women like her with earnest intentions with such ease. She was not the sort to enrapture a man. The chances he wanted anything but a chance liaison at best and a cruel lesson to be taught to a scribbler at worst were nil.

And yet, she did not have any alternatives, not at present. Lavinia had never been in a position to try to net a husband before, and, being born in a middlingly comfortable position in the world and freed from the need of a spouse's support by her pen, she only saw the world of female desperation from a distance. She saw it well and clear; indeed, she portrayed it in ruthless details in her debut on a young lady's entry in the world.

But it was one thing to see and to know and another to feel the humiliation in her blood. To realise she simply had to take a chance with a man who most probably was no less a rake than Lord Granville, if not more so, because otherwise she might miss a chance at a serious courtship, and then all hope would be lost with it.

She did not formulate these thoughts in perfect sentences, like lines upon lines in a lady's diary. They flashed through her head as an angry, degrading mixture. She nodded and resumed her seat.

'Tsk, is that a seemly conduct for a young woman?' Mrs Schwellenberg asked almost as quietly as the dark-haired rogue had when he invited Lavinia to the library.

Lavinia froze. 'Whatever do you mean?' She tried to conceal her nerves. She hoped the older lady had not overheard her secret agreement. Unfortunately, she was in a perfect position to overhear it since she was sitting only two steps away from Lavinia.

'I mean, Miss Dudley, that you seem to be losing all sense of shame. What kind of a young woman with any sense of proper conduct fetches her own fan from the floor?' The hue of the last words was such as though she said it from the gutter.

Lavinia sighed. The relief was such it set her head spinning as if her veins were suddenly drained of blood. 'Do forgive me,' she said meekly, the very picture of a dutiful slipper fetcher. 'It was my uncouth upbringing rearing its head once again.'

'Are you looking for something, young man?' The proprietor of the circulating library addressed Hugh with respect without deference. A man keeping such an establishment in a modish place like Cheltenham, one who had already lived through one royal visit before, must have been fairly accustomed to visitors in well-tailored clothes and tight cravats.

Yes, Hugh thought. *I am looking for the woman who doesn't seem to be able to keep herself out of trouble.*

Aloud, however, he merely said, 'Thank you, Mr Harward. I am merely thinking.'

'Are you sure? We have splendid quarto editions of the best histories, not to mention books on divinity…' The elderly proprietor paused, evidently deciding a young buck of the court was unlikely to be interested in such lofty theological matters, and he added, 'We have the latest novels, too.'

'Do you have Dudley's *Miranda*, too?' Hugh asked, not without some impishness on his mind.

'Oh, I'm so sorry, Mr—'

'Lord Granville.'

Hugh had no idea why he was at Mr Harward's library at this hour. If someone had asked him why he was there, he would have unlikely been at a loss for words, a situation unfamiliar to him. But whether he would have replied something approaching truth – or even admitted as much to himself – was another matter. Upon thinking about it, his response would most likely be something about being bored senseless of what passed for drama in Cheltenham, if yesterday's evening was any indication, and wanting to see some real thing.

The truth was that he didn't like Kurt von Wallmoden's whispers one bit. There was sense in the saying that it takes one to know one, and if Hugh was ever anything approaching a rake – or, at least, what passed for a rake at this prudish court – he knew the royal relative was no family man either. For one thing, he didn't have a family. Not that the possession of a wife ever prevented men of the ton from seeking diversions elsewhere, but to keep things fair, the same things could be said of the wives.

That was not the kind of world Hugh wanted Lavinia Dudley to enmesh herself in. His plan was to play Cupid for a change and sneak her into matrimonial bliss under the nose of the Cerberus that watched her – not to make her into a nobleman's mistress.

For one thing, one had to have some sympathy for the nobleman. She was like to bore him stiff by reading him lectures on proper decorum in bed and attempting to regulate his consumption of port outside it.

'I'm so sorry, your lordship. She is ever popular, and I don't think we have a copy left at the moment. Now, if you were to wait until someone returned one…'

'It's a shame she hasn't written a new piece for so long.' Hugh glanced at the door. The courting couple was to appear at any moment. He wasn't sure why the smooth proceeding of his plan irritated him to no end. Perhaps, it was because he knew that such interest as Kurt von Wallmoden expressed in the dowriless authoress did not necessarily lead down the aisle.

'Oh, yes. But who can blame her? Even ladies of unimpeachable virtue sometimes succumb.'

'Whatever do you mean?'

'There is talk on the street that she had come to court to find a husband and found herself a gentleman protector instead.'

'What an utter Banbury tale!' Hugh exclaimed. 'Even if someone offered Miss Dudley such a thing, she never would have agreed to it.'

'Why would they not have offered it? I've never seen her, but, by all accounts, she is a pretty young woman.'

Hugh opened his mouth to deny this allegation and then paused. Lavinia Dudley was no ravishing beauty, that was true; she would never lay waste to a ballroom full of suitors with a glance. The slow and ceremonious manner imposed on her by court did not lend her any allure either, at least from Hugh's perspective; he had little time for the kind of pastel-coloured misses extolled by conduct books. But she had a pleasant face, white arms, a softness to her features, eyes of bright blue...and, most of all, there was something unnameable – something smouldering beneath the iron regimen. Hugh recalled the evening of the concert and her vehement denials of needing any help. Her words were nonsensical – and infuriating – but there was a kind of fire in her eyes no decorum could conceal.

'She is pretty,' he finally said. 'She is...quite remarkably pretty, in fact. But there is no woman I've ever known who conducted herself with greater regard for her reputation. If gossips in the street seek to attach the name of a lightskirt to someone, let them look someplace else.'

'You are quite a vehement defender of the fair sex I see, your lordship.'

No, I am not. I am the last person ladies should call upon for defence.

'If you are acquainted with Miss Dudley,' Mr Harward continued, 'could you pass my wife's regards to her? Margaret had read and reread *Miranda* at least a dozen times by now and claims the resolution of the plot brings her great solace. She has lent the copy to our daughter, too, and now they speak in the cryptic language of quotes that excludes me from the conspiracy.'

'You haven't read her novel yourself, then?'

'Modern novels are not to my taste. Richardson I can abide but only in a certain mood. Usually, I read the Romans.'

'You should make an exception for Miss Dudley and heed not the rumours.'

'Can you blame the gossips? She hasn't written another work for two years by now. It's not the height of unreason to suppose she might have found herself another occupation.'

'Her only occupation so far has been serving Her Majesty.' *Otherwise known as the prissy German creature in voluminous robes and a fortress of prudery.* 'Her thoughts are occupied by nothing else.'

'If you insist, your lordship.'

'You of all people should know the difference between the truth and the fable.'

Hugh was surprised by his own stubbornness. Was it Miss Dudley's dark influence, turning him into a bore? Any other time, any other woman, he would have laughed at the notion that such a rule-abiding creature could be thought to be someone's voluptuous mistress. Perhaps, he would have even supplied an outlandish tale or two himself, just for the lark of it.

But it was not the same with Miss Dudley. She was almost his protégé now. Her fine feelings were a different matter. He didn't mind puncturing her sense of the proper himself, sometimes, but it was different if someone else tried to do it. Utterly different. He felt rather proprietor-like over the feelings in question.

There was a shuffle of familiar feet behind him and the sound of the door being closed. Without turning toward the newcomers, Hugh said, ' 'Actually, I very much would like to look at your rare quartos. Do you happen to have any in the back rooms?'

Chapter 5

Lavinia would have lied if she said she felt no trepidation at coming to Mr Harward's. True, a circulating library was a daylit, public place and one where few people would have suspected even a court pair of debauchery. But still, she knew how fleeting the attentions of highborn gentlemen could be. Not on her own skin, of course, thank God. She had always been too careful to enmesh herself in such situations, but she had read and heard enough tales of woe.

She had written a whole novel on the subject of fine lines between propriety and ruin. She knew she had to choose her words carefully.

When Lavinia saw Lord Granville engaged in a conversation with the man who was presumably Mr Harward, she froze. There was no possibility at all that his visit to the library was an accident. He must have overheard her conversation with Kurt von Wallmoden at the theatre and decided to follow her.

Whatever was his reason? Lavinia wasn't about to think even for a minute that the golden-haired rake cared a whit about her safety and had come here for her sake. At best, he was worried she would not be able to conduct the conversation well on her own and thought he would need to interject; at worst,.. eavesdropping on her tentative courtship was his idea of fun.

Lavinia was not about to give him any. She marched to one of the bookcases and turned to the neatly-ordered shelves. She avoided touching anything and pretended to be tremendously interested in the rows of sermons. It did not take long for a gentleman with dark hair and a mild German accent to join her.

'Miss Dudley.' Kurt von Wallmoden inclined his head in a barely perceptible gesture. 'Always a pleasure to see you.'

'I can say the same.'

'We don't have much time. I am expected at a vital engagement. So, let us be clear.' He touched the spine of Fordyce's *Sermons to Young Women* without much ceremony. 'I think I know of your predicament.'

'Do you?'

'You're unhappy at court. You want an escape.' His whisper was low. 'I can provide you with it.'

Lavinia whipped her head around, looking at him face to face. Her brain refused to believe the frankness of his words. It couldn't have been that easy. Her life might have been sheltered after a fashion, but even she knew nothing one desired simply fell into one's lap like an overripe fruit. Especially if one was a woman – however young, however pretty, however fine her newly made clothes.

'You are very generous, Herr von Wallmoden,' Lavinia said cautiously. 'Especially given my...station in life.'

'Your station in life is an asset.'

'Is it?' The cogs in her mind were whirring. Was he trying to horrify the ton by finding himself the most unsuitable bride possible? Was he trying to conceal some vice by a hasty marriage? Was he so deep in debt that genuinely well-portioned women refused to countenance him as a husband?

'Of course. After all, you flit beneath everyone's notice. Everyone at this court is watching everyone else, that is true, but you are watched much less than others are. A second keeper of the robes... Forgive me, but it is no exalted title.'

Lavinia saw clearly that he didn't mean to wound her. He was merely observing the reality, and her station in life was as much a reality as the blue colour of the sky. A wise thing to do would have been to perceive it as no slight and accept it graciously. So why on earth did it sting so much?

'No.' Lavinia turned her face away to the books again. 'No, it is not. But in that case, your offer is all the stranger.'

'You have not heard my offer yet.'

'Are there so many options?'

'You may be surprised, Miss Dudley. You may be very well surprised.'

Something must have reflected on her face, for the next thing she heard was Kurt von Wallmoden's low, soft laughter. You couldn't have thought that I was going to ask for your hand, could you?'

"Of course not.' Lavinia did her best to reply with dignity. 'The thought entered my mind but only as an example of something utterly preposterous.'

'That speaks well of your sense. I don't need your charms, Miss Dudley. I need your modesty. Your quiet ways. In short, I need your assistance.'

'Assistance in what?'

'There is a young lady who came to my notice during the last royal visit to Cheltenham. I should very much like to renew our acquaintance.'

'Why on earth would you need my assistance in courtship?'

'The lady is no pauper but not the sort of woman Their Majesties might have in mind for me either. You know the gossips of the court. Such things need to be managed discreetly.'

Lavinia did not ask what he meant by such things. She merely looked at him, prompting him silently. This, she knew, was one of the better ways to draw words out of people without looking too determined. Eldest daughters learnt plenty of such tricks when growing up.

The dark-haired nobleman did not resist that insistent gaze any more than her father or stepmother ever did. 'Letters. Trinkets. I need a trustworthy go-between to pass such things on. If everything goes well, I promise to hint to Her Majesty that it may be better if you were released from her service.'

'If everything goes well?' Lavinia could not manage the sharpness in her voice. She sensed all too well the solid universe behind these four words.

'If my acquaintance with Miss Peabody reaches a happy conclusion.'

Somehow, being now able to put a name to the nebulous figure of his victim-to-be made Lavinia feel worse. 'I am not going to assist in someone's seduction and ruin,' she said flatly, trying to still the angry shivering in her hands.

'Such dreadful words. Did you read them in a novel?'

'You are forgetting yourself, Herr von Wallmoden.'

'No, I'm afraid it is you who is forgetting yourself – or, rather, forgetting the truth of your situation. Remember, Miss Dudley, if I can influence Her Majesty to let you go, I can just as well tell her that you are an incomparable ornament and the court simply cannot do without you.'

'You will not do it only because I refused your scheme—'

'It is not your place to tell me what I can and cannot do.'

'I...'

'She means to say' – another man joined the conversation, his voice sounding assured and bright even when lowered to a manageable whisper – 'that she agrees to your offer.'

Lavinia turned on her heel and saw Lord Granville standing behind her, leaning in as though he was a part of this dispute. As though it were his decision to make. As though it was his soul to sell. 'I absolutely do not!' she hissed, forgetting her manners for a moment. 'Lord Granville, I think you've rendered me quite enough assistance!'

'It's always a pleasure to deal with reasonable people,' Kurt von Wallmoden commented. 'Granville, I trust you'll be able to bring your little friend here to her senses?'

'She has merely been overwhelmed by the generosity of your offer,' Lord Granville replied cheerfully.

For a second, Lavinia wanted to claw his eyes out as though she were some wild hoyden from a comedic play. 'Do you even realise what he is asking of us?' she asked angrily. 'Of me?'

'Of course. It's not to murder an orphan, though judging by your tone one might've thought otherwise. It's to assist the course of love.'

'Love! You are merely mocking me. You know as well as I do that love has nothing to do with it.'

'Miss Dudley, lovers have passed notes and gifts to each other since times immemorial. Ovid writes about it quite vividly.'

'I haven't read Ovid,' Lavinia said with all the hauteur she could muster. In truth, she found there was little pride to be found in not having read something, however scandalous the material, but she was not about to have Lord Granville know it.

'I should lend you my copy. It's a very instructional read. There is nothing outrageous in what Herr von Wallmoden wants to do. It's not as though he is planning to waylay and force the poor thing. He would be merely giving her a choice. She might send the trinkets away, should she wish to, and then goodness will triumph, and angels shall rejoice.'

'What if she doesn't?'

'What poor opinion do you have of the mysterious Miss Peabody!' Lord Granville was plainly enjoying himself now. 'Think of it – what value does her virtue have, if it's not battle-tested? Have you ever heard of a saint who has never encountered temptation? It would be like calling someone a great warrior because he never faced an enemy attack.'

'What a way with words you have, your lordship.'

'From a woman of your talent, I'd take it as a compliment.'

'If you so wish,' Lavinia said, making it plain it wasn't intended as such.

'Most likely, even if the lady had known him before, she would have recognised with years that such an acquaintance can bring her naught but grief, and is probably going to reply to his letters with about the same expression as you are giving me now. Only rendered into written word.'

That was certainly possible, Lavinia couldn't help but acknowledge. If Miss Peabody had a sensible bone in her body, she was likely to do just that. But in that case... She turned to the son of the royal bastard, her cheeks still hot. 'You told me you are going to help me only if your *courtship* reaches a happy conclusion. What if Miss Peabody refuses you?'

'It's a good question.' Lord Granville intervened yet again. 'What is Miss Dudley going to get in that case?'

'How will I know Miss Dudley was not the one who influenced her in that direction?' Kurt von Wallmoden asked, not without reason, for that was precisely what Lavinia was now secretly hoping to do.

'I am going to watch over her,' Lord Granville replied as though that was the most natural thing in the world. 'We shall be joined at the hip like a sister and a brother as long as this mission lasts.'

'I will trust you if you give me your word as a gentleman.'

'I would.'

The sickening irony of that demand, as long as Lavinia was concerned, was something worthy of a satirical novel.

'In that case,' Kurt von Wallmoden said, 'I promise to render my assistance as soon as Their Majesties return from Cheltenham, provided you carry out every task I give you. Not before and not in any other instance. What do you think of that, Miss Dudley?'

The question was a silken sham. He wasn't interested in what she thought of these conditions, for he was not going to offer any other alternative.

Lavinia felt as though the walls of unseen castle walls – ancient walls, walls breathing dark histories – were closing in on her. She was standing in the daylight, in an open, modern room made airy with high ceilings and decorated with antique busts, and yet she felt like the heroine of one of her tortured tragedies.

Perhaps, it had always been like this, for each generation of silent court ladies, the companions to the queen – since the days of half-nameless medieval consorts and the bloody Tudor wives. Countless women to give their mistresses slippers and prayer books, to fetch shawls for them and keep their sleep, and then disappear into the shadows.

But unlike them, Lavinia Dudley, the child of an enlightened age, had a way out. The way out was standing right in front of her. She was going to resolve this dilemma somehow. She was going to carry out the devilish task without sullying her conscience forever. She only needed to find a way.

'Very well,' Lavinia said, her fingertips touching Fordyce, almost feeling the regiment of sermons on proper attire and chaste conduct marching inside. 'I will help you, Herr von Wallmoden.'

'But' –once again, Lord Granville answered for Lavinia before she opened her mouth – 'you must give Miss Dudley a promise that you are going to uphold your part of the bargain.'

'Indeed,' the other man replied. 'I give you my word as a gentleman.'

'You really didn't have to pay for my subscription to the assembly rooms,' Lavinia Dudley whispered as Hugh led her into the hot, cramped ballroom that was the shining centre of Cheltenham's genteel society.

'It was only half a guinea.'

'I could afford it. I do draw wages as the second keeper of the robes.'

It was obvious Miss Dudley was in a huff tonight. The reason was not difficult to divine either. Tonight was her first task, or maybe it was their first task, for Kurt von Wallmoden. A note was to be passed to Miss Peabody from her highborn admirer.

Even in a huff, Miss Dudley looked exquisite, shining with the kind of pale intensity even the corseted life of the court couldn't dim. It was this radiance, the looks of a silver-skinned virgin from a Continental fresco, that first drew Hugh to her on the night of the royal ball.

'I do wonder which one of them is Miss Peabody,' he said, steering his thoughts consciously away from Miss Dudley. 'It's a shame she is not of so grand a rank as to have had her portrait painted.'

'Had she been of so grand a rank, she would not have attracted his attention,' Miss Dudley said with nervous archness. She clearly avoided using Kurt von Wallmoden's name – or the name of any participant in this scheme – aloud. 'After all, great ladies are protected by their families. Miss Peabody, I imagine, has no one.'

'Do you think she lives on the street, then? In that case, it's strange she would be admitted to the upper assembly rooms.'

'You are joking again.'

'Guilty as charged. Besides, she has an aunt. He mentioned as much.'

'An aunt would not fight a duel for your honour.'

'That depends on the aunt.'

Hugh had barely finished speaking when he heard a faint, ladylike laughter. The source of the sound was not far, and when he turned his head in that direction, he glimpsed the most exquisite redhead he had ever seen.

Petite, grey-clad and grey-eyed, she would not have been all that different from the other misses populating the assembly rooms on the night of the Friday ball, had it not been for the violent red of her hair. It seemed to be burning like a crown of flame.

The young woman met his gaze frankly. Then, as though recalling some unwritten rule, she lowered her eyes in a show of modesty.

'Miss Dudley,' Hugh said, 'I believe we have found our quarry.'

Engineering an introduction through the master of ceremonies was not the most difficult task Hugh had ever encountered. If anything, it was as easy as opening a well-oiled door. Not so much because of who he was, necessarily, or even because of his title and an estate whose lands were not far from here, but because he was now known to be a part of the court. The royal court was the place from which all nobility and generosity of the land flowed and granted all the blessings to the town it deigned to visit.

The girl's aunt, introduced to him as Mrs Atwell, nodded politely at Lavinia; however, Hugh captured her undivided attention. All that was required of him was to think up a word of praise for her charge's conduct.

'Lord Granville,' she gushed, 'what a great honour you do us with your compliment! Madeline, do not stand as though a pillar of salt – thank his lordship.'

Madeline Peabody murmured a word of thanks, gently and quietly. She raised her eyes from the floor and looked at him with demure doe eyes – eyes almost too perfect to be true.

Lavinia fidgeted by his side. The note was hidden in her sleeve, but she could not pass it on to Miss Peabody while her guardian was watching. Lord Granville,' she said, 'I do believe a new allemande is starting.'

'Do you have a liking for the music?'

'I always did.'

That surprised him. He had always thought the proper and studious Miss Dudley had much preferred the cotillions of court balls, not the lively music of the assembly rooms. He imagined her skipping around in a reel or a good country dance, her ankles, already daringly apt to be glimpsed by those new gowns of hers, bared blithely with every jump. Dancing was an energetic pastime – even more energetic than bedsport, in his experience – although, of course, both depended on the partner, and her face would probably be flushed in no time. Hugh wondered how that pretty shade of crimson would look against her pale-gold hair.

'So does Madeline,' Mrs Atwell interjected. 'She is a very accomplished dancer.'

Hugh saw something insistent in Lavina's eyes. 'Do forgive me, Mrs Atwell,' Hugh said with all the charm he could muster, 'but Miss Dudley has already promised me the first dance. I would be honoured, however, to invite your niece for the second.'

'You are most kind, your lordship,' Madeline Peabody whispered, her grey eyes soft. 'I am glad to accept your invitation.'

The musicians struck the first note of the allemande. The master of ceremonies beamed as soon as he saw Hugh and Lavinia take hands, and he gestured for them to step forward as the leading couple.

Wasn't that wonderful? Nothing to excite the blood like conducting secret dealings in the bright-lit heart of a ballroom. Usually, Hugh was all in favour of anything that excited the blood. He couldn't help but notice the stiffening of Miss Dudley's expression. Not so much disapproval as terror. Her sharing of his taste didn't go so far as this. That was quite a shame.

Keeping the smile on his lips, Hugh took her hand in preparation for leading the dance. It was the first time, it occurred to him, he could do so. It was peculiar he hadn't touched her flesh yet even through the chaste gloves. He had been in her room, her inner sanctum as well as a place of sleep and work, but he had never touched her. Her palm in his hand was hot and sweaty.

'Worry not,' he murmured as they moved through the ballroom. 'It's all going to go smoothly as butter.'

'Do you feel no regret that it will?' Miss Dudley replied just as quietly.

In lieu of an answer, Hugh set her spinning. The spring-green gown immediately rose in a whirl of colour, her ankles thin and slender beneath it. Hugh blinked and willed himself to look away. The scheme that had started as a diversion already had enough complications.

'Though I imagine you don't.' Lavinia was breathing quickly, her cheeks indeed tinged with a little pink now. Her voice was acid with disapproval, but she was looking at him with those widened eyes that bespoke excitement. 'I imagine you have quite a dozen of Madelines in your own past.'

'Perhaps, I do. But they were not unmarried damsels. None of them were, in fact.'

'Truly?' She blinked, the movement of her arms a bit tardy compared to his more practiced figures. 'None?'

'You might be surprised, Miss Dudley, but I gain no pleasure from ruining women's lives.'

There was such profound doubt in her expression that Hugh almost felt insulted.

'I may be a rake, as you have doubtless heard.' He leaned closer, her face only a few inches from his now. He could see the pale blue of her eyes disintegrate into multiple flecks and shades of blue. 'But a finished scoundrel I am not.'

'I hope you understand if I thought you a man more...careless with his pleasures.' She still sounded angry.

What on earth was the matter with her? Did she disapprove of every kind of night shared between those not husband and wife? Unless... No, that was impossible. His Lavinia Dudley, his silver-skinned virgin from a mural, could not have possibly been jealous.

'Oh, I promise you, Miss Dudley, when the situation calls for it, I can be very careful with my pleasures indeed.'

She was flushed now, and he could wager Granville Hall against a rented lodging in Covent Garden that dancing had only a little to do with it. Miss Dudley pressed the paper into his palm when their hands interlocked next. She did so in a hurry as though her task required her to touch open flames.

Miss Peabody was waiting for him to lead her into the next dance when his dance with Miss Dudley ended. She said little when Hugh took her hand; she said less through the first set of figures. She danced much better than Miss Dudley, Hugh noticed. More gracefully so, at any rate.

But, he supposed, when one was the daughter of a squire – even one who was unwise with his fortune and unlucky with sons who could have safeguarded what was left of it – she could concentrate all her energies of crafting herself into a perfection of marriageability.

'How did you meet His Majesty's nephew?' Hugh asked when the perfection in question stopped her whirling. Nephew sounded much more genteel than half-nephew by a bastard brother and took less time to say.

'During the first royal visit to Cheltenham,' Miss Peabody replied, her smile unchanging. 'My father was still alive then. I was one of the ladies selected to meet the party…'

Hugh could imagine it well. From what he had heard, Simeon Moreau, who was selected as the master of ceremonies for the whole visit back then, was in charge of attending to Their Majesties as well as to the less distinguished members of the royal family. It was not difficult to suppose he drew the prettiest flowers of the local squires and gentry in order to ornament the welcome.

'I see,' Hugh said. 'Did you curtsy before him in a particularly exquisite way?'

'I presented him with an embroidery. His family crest.' She smiled. 'Three rams and a helmet of black and gold.'

It was no wonder von Wallmoden was captivated by her. For the younger son of a bastard, orbiting a court much more glittering than that of his own family's, it must have been heady to encounter such breathless regard. Besides, he did not doubt that Miss Peabody's needlework, like everything else about her, was careful and well-executed.

When he passed the note into her palm, she grasped it as though it were a rope thrown to someone drowning. The smile never left her lips.

Chapter 6

'**G**ranville?'

The familiar voice sounded incredulous. Hugh turned and saw Sir Stephen Prescott, the companion of his childhood, who was a keen horseman with broad shoulders.

'Guilty as charged,' Hugh replied, looking at Sir Stephen Prescott.

'I didn't expect to see you here.'

Hugh raised his eyebrows. 'I can take myself away if the sight is displeasing to you.'

'Ever joking, aren't you? I have heard of the royal visit, but I could not imagine you would have any desire to visit the Friday ball here. You must be used to better ballrooms by now. More exalted company, too.'

More exalted company? Hugh thought of his fellow equerries with their arts of careful dancing around the issue of the king's illness – a dancing with more elaborate figures than any he had seen here tonight. He thought of the aristocratic ladies-in-waiting, silent by their queen's side. He thought of the strange isolation of the place, its existence to the rhythm of its own internal clocks.

Exalted company for sure. There was something in it of the rarefied air of a monastery high in the snow-capped mountains.

He wasn't about to say any of that to his old friend, nor even ruminate on it overmuch himself. He had a duty to his family name, and the duty was what he was going to fulfil. When Miss Dudley was going to flit out of the court with the same peculiar chance that made her enter it in the first place, she would betray no one's memory. If he were to do so, it would be another matter entirely.

'I am here for Miss Dudley's sake.' He didn't lie, technically. 'Though I would've come still, had I known you are frequenting the town now.'

'Forgive me – would you mind introducing your lady to me?'

'Of course. Miss Dudley, this is Sir Stephen Prescott, a man I had the honour of calling my friend ever since his family came to visit Granville Hall at my tender age of nine. Sir Stephen, this is Lavinia Dudley who is...likewise my good friend.' That explanation would do. *A good friend.* Such a murky definition when it came to pretty young women.

Sir Stephen's face lit up as though he had bagged a particularly plump partridge on an autumn hunt. 'A good friend, I see! Well, I have always thought it's high time you had a good friend and companion. I don't believe I have heard of your family.' Sir Stephen looked closely at her. 'You are not of the Northumberland Dudleys, by any chance?'

A smile touched Miss Dudley's lips at the notion that she could be descended from the famed family that produced the dukes of Warwick.

'She is one of the ladies who serve Her Majesty,' Hugh said quickly, sidestepping the question. It was confusing enough that Sir Stephen thought her Hugh's bride-to-be. It would be worse if he heard the novelist's no doubt painfully honest answer and later took him aside to ask Hugh what was he thinking, courting a girl with nothing but loveliness to recommend her.

Loveliness and talent and more unbending morals than any he had encountered in any young woman – or young man – of the ton or the court alike. *Stubbornness, also. And a great gift at eating oneself alive.*

'That's splendid. It's a shame your old man isn't here to see Miss Dudley, isn't it? I remember he was always trying to find you a good match with this neighbour's girl or that. Of course, if he had been here, you wouldn't have been at court. Of course, he loved Granville Hall, but—'

'Prescott. This is quite enough. I am sure Miss Dudley isn't interested in these old tales.'

'I wouldn't say they are so old. But let no one claim that Stephen Prescott doesn't take a hint.'

His friend had always had all the tact and subtlety of a boar. Hugh was already feeling Lavinia Dudley's anxious, curious stare upon himself.

The sensation was not unpleasant, oddly enough. It was only a shame she was only attracted to the murky waters behind Sir Stephen's words and not to anything to do with Hugh himself.

Given that the moral harness she imposed upon herself was hardly less strict than that of Queen Charlotte herself, it was highly unlikely she ever would be.

'What happened to your father?' Lavinia asked as they stepped out upon the balcony. They were not alone – two young women, sisters by the looks of them, were laughing in the other corner, so Lavinia had no fears regarding the propriety of the situation. Now she would only have to speak in a low, soft voice, so as to avoid anyone eavesdropping.

Fortunately, the years at court had taught her this skill whether she wanted to learn it or not.

'He died, Miss Dudley. A sadly common fate for men his age.'

'You are jesting still. I've heard your friend. He couldn't have meant death alone.'

'Why not?'

'Why did your father live out his last years at his estate if he was such a brilliant courtier?' Lavinia knew she was prying, and she knew it was not right. But there was something about this man, this co-conspirator of hers, that made her natural passions – be that curiosity or anger – well up, drowning propriety in their wake.

'Brilliant courtiers rarely stay brilliant courtiers all their lives. Read any account of the lives of those who were close to Good Queen Bess or her father.'

'I've read plenty of them,' Lavinia parried. 'Surely you aren't going to tell me that your father had been exiled for plotting with the Spanish?'

'Of course not. We live in a more genteel age, after all, don't we?' The conversation with Sir Stephen must have torn at something in him, for there was now an unmistakable ire in his voice. 'We have smaller crimes.'

'Then he did nothing so terrible.'

'Not if you ask Her Majesty's opinion on the matter.'

'Queen Charlotte? Was it her who exiled him?'

'Of course not. She is such a proper wedded wife, after all, and would never dream of usurping her husband's power in these matte rs... she would simply whisper in his ear. If he abides by her whispers, who can blame him?'

'Lord Granville,' Lavinia stepped closer, and put her hand upon his arm. 'What has your father done?'

'Nothing. Nothing that merited his fall. He was protecting a woman he knew since she was a girl.'

'His intended?'

'No. Caroline Mathilde.'

'Who...' Lavinia realised where she had heard this name. The night, the terror, the ramblings of a mad king. *Do you remember what happened to poor Mathilde when father sent her away?*

'King George's sister. The one who went to Denmark. I trust you know her story? There was a time, Father said, it was thrumming through every chamber at court.' Upon seeing Lavinia shake her head, he added, 'Though, I suppose, for most people, it's old news now. Yesterday's papers. She died in Celle not long after you were born, after all. Or me, for that matter. But it was, by the end of 'Father's life, the only story it seemed he had left in him to tell.'

'Can you tell it to me now?' Lavinia asked quietly.

'It's a long tale. Very Bard-like, in its way. It does sometimes seem to belong to the days of Good Queen Bess.'

'Or her father?'

'Perhaps especially her father. I told you Her Majesty is not the sort of woman to try and usurp her husband's power – well, Caroline Mathilde, Queen Caroline Mathilde as she was by then, was precisely that sort of woman. It's not right, not usually, but her husband was a brute and a madman and not a benevolent madman like His Majesty either. She found a lover, a court physician. An enlightened man, everyone said, as enlightened as she was accomplished. They seized the throne together. She made him regent. He made her a queen reigning, not a consort weeping in the shadows as she was before.

'An outrageous woman, Father said, and he used to know her as a boisterous young girl. As I grew, some of his tales prickled my blood more than others did. When he told me how she, as queen, used to ride the streets of Copenhagen incognito in a man's garments and take part in archery contests, I thought God, how I wish I could have bedded this woman.'

'Lord Granville!'

'What's the matter, Miss Dudley? You have blood enough to hear about high treason but not about matters of the flesh?'

'How did it all end?'

'Bloodily, of course. Both arrested after a masked ball. The physician was tortured for confession and then broken on the wheel, still wearing the finery from the fete. I did tell you it was a dark, old-fashioned tale. You aren't pale, I see.'

'I've read worse in Titus Andronicus.'

'You are ready to faint at impropriety but not at the mention of executions. You're a curious thing.'

'I do not faint at impropriety. I merely dislike it.'

'Why so?'

'Because I am afraid of it.' The words were out of her mouth before she could stop them.'

Something changed in Lord Granville's expression, and the brief levity sank back into the swamp. 'As it turns out, Queen Caroline Mathilde should have been more afraid of it still. She was to be sent back to her brother's domain after she was dethroned by her own mother-in-law.'

'That doesn't seem such a dire fate to me. She must have longed for her days of girlhood sometimes.'

Oftentimes, Lavinia wished her own girlhood continued indefinitely. It was comfortable to her to remain a flitting shadow, glowing by her father's side. Much, much better than being at the centre of attention as the mistress of a household.

'It wouldn't have been a dire fate, no. Except it didn't come to pass. Her Majesty claimed she would rather lie down and die on the spot than allow that amoral woman into the same court as her virginal, pure little daughters. She coaxed and coaxed, pleaded and pleaded, until her royal husband agreed and forbade his own sister her own native shores. Her Majesty didn't even want him to allow her Hanover – its court, after all, was known for loose morals, and who knew what mischief a woman of spirit and ambition could wreak there? No. She made sure her disgraced in-law went to Celle.'

'Celle. I think I know the name. Isn't it the place where...' Something scratched at the edges of Lavinia's mind; some gothic tale so distant it gained almost mythological outlines.

'Where the very first King George imprisoned his discarded wife until her death? Yes, the very one. Father was against sending Queen Caroline Mathilde there. He tried to talk His Majesty out it even though he knew his royal wife will not like the interference. He failed. His Majesty's sister died in Celle, not yet thirty. And Father was exiled from court as soon as Her Majesty could contrive it. She does not forget, that one. And she does not forgive.'

'How did you become a royal equerry, then?'

'The summons arrived a mere month after 'Father's death. I was as surprised as you are, but I've heard whispers since. Hints that His Majesty, in one of his lucid moments, regretted his old friend's exile and death and wanted to make amends to his son. Give our family another chance.'

'You came to the court that cost your father his position and possibly his life?'

'I am the only son of the Granvilles. I have no living brothers. The proximity to the throne was what gave father his standing and wealth, before the former was snatched away. Who is going to repair it if not me?'

'I would have never thought you to be a man so caught up in duty.'

'Why on earth else do you suppose I accepted the position, let alone remained in it? Do you suppose I so enjoy spending my life making a king who dreams of dead friends walking and invents illusions for his wife presentable to the public? Do you imagine taking daily turns on the terrace with him is what I dreamed about when I was a boy?'

'"If the position at court is so crucial to you, why are you jeopardising it by...' A realisation suddenly pierced Lavinia's brain, and it was as though a bucket of icy water was upturned upon her whole person. 'Your plan,' she said slowly. 'Your desire to get me away from the court... It was to be a little revenge, wasn't it? Rob Queen Charlotte of her prized pet. Not quite an equal reckoning for what she did to your father but a fine little twist still.'

'I've always thought you were a clever thing.'

'You wanted to make use of me.'

'I wanted to make a trade with you. My assistance for yours.'

'A goodly trade it is if the other merchant doesn't know the contents of the sack!'

'Are you such an ardent admirer of Her Majesty's virtue that these contents disgust you?'

'I...'

Had this conversation happened but a few months or even hours ago, Lavinia would have replied that she was – vehemently so. But now she was at a loss for words; worse, she was at a loss for a firm decision in her own mind. Lord Granville had no reason to lie to her. If what Lord Granville told her was true, that meant Queen Charlotte was not simply a woman of stark purity herself, not simply a woman demanding the same of those around her, but also the kind of woman who would deny an exile what was essentially her family home for these principles. The kind of woman who would ruin a man for opposing them and her.

Lavinia wasn't about to throw her allegiances to the wind. After all, if she did, it would have meant she had spent those last strangling her own discontent, smothering her feelings, and silencing her voice for an empty honour. That would have been too much. She was, however, shaken sufficiently to hesitate with her reply.

Lord Granville smirked. 'I knew they didn't. You are a clever thing, as I've said. You have a mind of your own even if you need to be angered to bring it out.'

'You are an impertinent, disrespectful—'

Lord Granville snaked an arm around her waist, pulled her close, and kissed her on the mouth. A wave of panic crashed over Lavinia's head. She glimpsed, to the left, an empty balcony – the laughing sisters must have long since gone inside. The fact should have alarmed Lavinia more. She was now alone with a notorious rake and, should he try anything horrid, there would be no one to help – and, should someone intrude upon them and discover her in his grasp, she would be ruined.

She had never been kissed on the lips before and never had any desire for it. Little sensual disobediences of rebellious daughters were not for her. But now she wondered, I f that stemmed from genuine virtue or from the simple fact that no man worth disobedience had come her way in all these years. Lord Granville's kiss was certainly worth a disobedience. Heated and insistent, it was possibly worth a whole treason.

'His hands slid down her back and stopped at her waist – just as she had imagined him doing with his shadowy conquest the night she went to the queen. His fingers were warm like the spring twilight, and their warmth seemed to burn through the muslin and her shift, branding her skin beneath. He released her mouth and drew back, a kind of daze in his forest-green eyes.

The music from the rooms started again after a pause, and Lavinia became consciously aware of the couples whirling and skipping and jumping mere metres from where she was committing a heinous mistake.

For that was what it was – a heinous mistake. Women in her position, women without dowries and fragile in the world, had been ruined for less.

It was impossible Lord Granville didn't know that.

'Is it a further plan of revenge?' she asked, her voice still breathless and loathed herself for that breathlessness. 'To ruin the queen's reading pet if you won't be able to snatch her away?'

'Do you really think that I could look at you and think of something as cold and rational as revenge? Do you think any man could?'

'Yes. Because I am not, as you have yourself once informed me, a ravishing beauty. Revenge is the most logical reason someone would try to ruin someone like me.'

'Did I say that? I was a fool. You are ravishing to me. If other men disagree with me, it's their own blindness and does not concern me.'

'You cannot marry me, your lordship.' The address was a deliberate bit of coldness. 'You've all but said it. You need to repair your family's position at court. You would need a highborn wife for that. If you intended to dally with me without marrying, then you are a worse cad than I thought and a liar besides since you've told me about your rules never to seduce unmarried women.'

'You overestimate my powers of rational thinking if you think that something as deliberate as intentions for the future entered my mind when I kissed you. But now that you lay it out, you are right, of course.' He stepped away from her, a bitter smile touching his soft lips. 'I promise, in the future, to only kiss married ladies.'

But the realisation they were alone, with no one to interrupt them, strangely emboldened her. After a second's hesitation, born of shock and inexperience, Lavinia found herself responding to his kiss.

Chapter 7

It was not that Hugh had never paid court to a woman prone to temptation; it was only that he had never done so on behalf of another man.

But the king's errant relative was clear. He could not be seen to visit the pretty Madeline himself. Therefore, it was up to Hugh, the greatly obliging Viscount Granville, to be the go-between.

Right now, Hugh did not feel especially obliging. However, there was naught else he could do. Infuriating through Miss Dudley was, he didn't want to jeopardise her chances of escape – and his own chances of seeing Her Majesty's face when her walking literary prize had to be given her resignation.

Infuriating, yes. That was the word for Lavinia Dudley. Strangely enough, she was less so when she was obviously, openly infuriated herself – her cheeks blazing and her eyes afire, and in those moments, she made him desire nothing so much as to spar with her forever.

Well, that and other things. It was when she was at her most saintly when he found himself wanting to tease her into life.

Other things indeed. She was not the kind of woman to agree to share his bed without marriage, nor would he earnestly ask her to since, unlike his married lovers, she lacked the protection of a husband's name. As he had told her, he might have been a rake, but a finished scoundrel he was not.

The kiss on the balcony was a moment of irresponsible weakness. She was, surprisingly so, right in that instance. It was never to be repeated again.

It was because of the combination of all those factors that Hugh now found himself knocking on the door of the modest, if well-situated, dwelling occupied by Miss Madeline Peabody and her widowed aunt.

He was received and admitted to the parlour. The interior surprised him: the textiles decorating the walls were cheap, but the windows were hung with what looked like a genuine brocatelle. A family of modest means but with aspirations.

The aunt was precisely the kind of retiring, dowdy creature he had expected. Miss Madeline, however... Now, she was not dowdy at all. The redhead was sipping her pekoe tea after her guardian poured the beverage for three with exquisite delicacy. Moreover, she was dressed in the kind of diaphanous gown Hugh had heard to be called chemise à la reine, that he saw actresses and duchesses wear at home. This kind of outfit could not be cheap. Neither was it particularly modest.

'It is so good to meet you, your lordship,' Mrs Atwell said. 'Who else can we rely on for the news from court? We have no other sources,' she added as though she had herself been a court lady only temporarily exiled from that place of bounty.

'There is nothing particularly noteworthy happening there these days,' Hugh replied. He knew how important it was sometimes to sustain others' illusions and not only from his experience of serving the mad king. 'Except...Her Majesty has a new second keeper of the robes. Lavinia Dudley serves her now in an honourable position.' This was not precisely news; Miss Dudley had taken up her post three years ago. He was not, however, sure they had heard of it.

'Miss Dudley! The romance authoress, isn't she? Well, I suppose she does have to do something useful once in a while. My Madeline reads no novels, your lordship.'

'Does she not? You must be a strict guardian.'

'It has nothing to do with me. She has no interest in the stuff and nonsense of this kind. She always knew what is good for her. Have you not, Madeline?'

'I hope so, dear aunt,' the young woman replied, putting the cup down. Her lips still wet from the tea, she ran her tongue over them as though catching the last drops.

Hugh felt the strangest sensation looking at her. He knew the gesture was as alluring as her gown, if not more so. However, he found himself watching it as though through a layer of cold glass, feeling nothing, desiring nothing.

Yes, the touch was as calculated as the professions of Miss Madeline's sensibility and dislike for novels. But calculation in women had never repelled him before. His mistresses were as calculating as could be.

The allure of Lavinia Dudley could not be running so deep as to render him immune to the charms of other ladies, could it?

'Madeline has recently celebrated her twentieth birthday,' Mrs Atwell said. 'His Majesty's visit to Cheltenham is, of course, the greatest gift she could have asked for.'

'I have always dreamed to catch one glimpse of him,' Madeline Peabody murmured softly. Her voice was like a mountain stream, pure and lovely.

If Hugh was to stay for too long, Mrs Atwell would probably prevail upon her niece to sing, and the way she sang would probably turn out to be divine.

You would not have liked the results, Hugh thought. He recalled all those mornings of fitting King George out for his famous stately walk upon the terrace and all those afternoons of nightmarish promenades in the garden, spent wondering if today was going to be a day of euphoric merriment for his royal charge or of such black melancholy Hugh would have cause to fear for His Majesty's life.

'He is a man of great kindness.' Hugh felt the habitual charming smile stretch his lips without a particle of change being occasioned within. 'A true father to his people.'

'Dear aunt,' Madeline said, turning to Mrs Atwell, 'I feel a little chilly. Would you mind bringing me my shawl?'

As ploys went, this one was not the most original one. Besides, it depended on the older woman not being terribly bright, for what intelligent woman would fall for such an obvious trick from a young woman wanting to be left alone with a handsome young man?

'Of course.' Mrs Atwell stood up. 'Do play the harpsichord while I'm gone, Madeline. I'm sure his lordship is going to love your accomplishment.'

This, too, was not a new thing. It did, however, prove Mrs Atwell was not as reckless as Hugh supposed her to be at first. This was not a large house, and one could reasonably hear the sound of music from another room. While the harpsichord kept playing, it would be clear the young woman was busy and nothing untoward was passing between her and their visitor.

Madeline Peabody obeyed, playing a ditty Hugh dimly remembered made popular by some play five years ago. However, once her aunt left the room, she turned sharply to Hugh. Have you brought something?' Madeline asked breathlessly. Her hands were still engaged, and she played without missing a note. She was accomplished indeed.

'"I did.' He took the gift in question out of his pocket.

The daylight streaming through the windows flared up upon the diamond bracelet. Madeline Peabody's eyes flashed almost as brightly as she saw the present.

'How sweet of him,' she murmured. 'God, but I missed Kurt so much. Put it in my pocket. It's here.' She nodded, rather generally, in the direction of her morning gown as a whole. 'Quickly.'

Fortunately for her, Hugh was sufficiently acquainted with female attire – with getting women out of it, mostly – to know where pocket holes were usually located. He slipped a hand in, depositing the thin piece of shining jewellery there. Madeline's flesh was burning through the thin linen as though her anticipation and frustrated desire lent themselves to her very body.

Hugh did not linger. Withdrawing his hand, he wondered if he slipped his fingers into Lavinia Dudley's secret pocket like this if her skin would feel just as heated through the cloth. She had no less a reason for frustration than Madeline Peabody did. More so, even.

When Mrs Atwell came back to the room with the shawl held aloft in her hands, he and Madeline were sitting innocently apart, as decorous as a Gainsborough portrait. She did take a lot of time for a simple errand, and it occurred to Hugh that, perhaps, she was hoping him to be a genuine suitor she could catch for her niece. The notion was not that laughable and would account for her desperation. Twenty was not thirty, but it was not seventeen, either.

It would also account for her curious tolerance of her niece's choice of attire. Everyone knew, after all, that a man with his blood up was not always a man thinking clearly. Hugh waited for quarter of an hour more and professed a hurry to make other morning calls.

'Your visit has been such a pleasure,' Mrs Atwell proclaimed. 'I would be so very delighted if you were to call upon us again while the court is in Cheltenham.'

'Oh, yes,' Madeline Peabody said, her voice as soft as before. 'We will both be delighted.'

When Hades freezes over. Hugh had been at wild parties organized by the imaginative Prinny; he had been in the bedchambers of shameless married noblewomen. But no visit before had given him such an acute desire to have a thorough bath.

Ladies of rank, as well as those fortunate enough to live within their orbit, had no need of the public spa room to drink the healing waters of Cheltenham's springs. Ladies of rank had access to the private wells of their peers, such as the sunken private well on Lord Fauconberg's residence. 'But no one could prevent, in this more louche atmosphere of a holiday, two young ladies-in-waiting from going to experience the atmosphere of a public place for the sheer thrill of it.

Likewise, when Lady Alicia and Lady Marianne invited Lavinia along with them, she was in no position to say no. In truth, she hoped for a quiet hour in the morning to work on reassembling the shambles of her writing or at least reading. That, however, was not to be.

One look at Lady Alicia was enough to freeze the blood in Lavinia's veins. Not because the young woman in question was unpleasant looking in any way – if anything, she was remarkably pretty. No,

Lavinia recognised in her the figure whose features she had only seen shrouded in shadows.

'She was the young lady-in-waiting from the night of the king's escape. That explained the invitation, Lavinia realised. They were now bound by shared fear. The night in question seemed to be three hundred years away as they were walking through the elm-lined avenue drenched in spring sunlight.

'Perhaps, we could go to Mr Cooke's porcelain warehouse next?' Lavinia ventured as she realised both were made too sullen by the lack of sleep to start the conversation. 'I've heard he has very fine exhibits.'

The women exchanged perplexed glances.

'But, Miss Dudley, his offerings are all Chinese!' Lady Alicia replied.

'Isn't that a good thing?' Lavinia asked. 'China being where porcelain originated to start with. That's why we also call it china.'

'Is it?' Lady Alicia turned to her friend.

'If Miss Dudley says it is so, she must be right,' the dark-haired Lady Marianne replied a little too meekly. 'She is the one for book learning, after all.'

'I cannot say I read that many books,' Lavinia lied hastily. It was not much of a lie these days, truly.

'Oh, but you must, Miss Dudley,' Lady Alicia said with what would have passed for earnestness, had Lavinia been more oblivious a creature. 'You write them, after all, and if you were not to write them, who is going to entertain Her Majesty these days?'

'Entertain. As though she was a jester from the old days while they were the legitimate companions. Lavinia's skin prickled as though from contact with some venom. 'Why do you dislike Chinese porcelain, anyhow?' She tried to return the conversation to its original, gentle topic.

'Oh, but it's so vulgar!' Lady Alicia exclaimed. 'All those men lounging about without a waistcoat, all those women sitting like tailors... 'Don't you think it vulgar, Marianne?'

'Terribly so. Though, I can imagine, Miss Dudley doesn't think so. It's vulgar compared to Dresden china, but I can't imagine she has seen much of it for comparison. Have you, Miss Dudley?'

The prickling became almost painful. The purpose of the excursion grew clear to her – clear as a blow to the head. It was not to bond with the woman who shared hours of fear with her. It was to make her understand the experience entitled her to no familiarity with the ladies who actually belonged at court. That the shared experience was an aberration. That she was to know her place.

'I have not,' Lavinia said softly. It cost her a great deal of effort – a greater deal, perhaps, than it would have before this trip.

It must have been that heady atmosphere of royal travels that imbalanced her so. Before that, Lavinia had lulled herself into the kind of numbness that would have allowed her now to bear the women's mockery almost easily. As it was, she barely restrained herself from telling them she saw no Dresden figurines in her childhood because she and her father both committed the great sin of getting where they were on the strength of their work. It was harder still to keep herself from saying she was so very sorry for them for not having parents who had accomplished the same.

'Why, not even in your father's study? I have heard he is a great admirer of all German things.'

'Not of all German things.' She knew what Lady Marianne was hinting at. One might have as well ripped the bandage off. 'Only the German music. He has been writing its history for a decade, and the third volume has recently gone to the printers.'

The two laughed as though they had heard an excellent joke. Lady Alicia shook her head. 'My, but you are quite a dynasty! The printers of London must be making quite a tidy sum off you.'

Here it came. Coup de grace, courtesy of Lady Alicia. No woman – or man, for that matter – of blood and breeding would ever deal with money in any way but the spending of it. That Lavinia and her father had done otherwise and were continuing to do so was unquestionable evidence of their inferiority.

Lavinia imagined how she might transfigure them in a novel she would one day write – one day when she would be safely away from court, walking in ease and leisure through a busy London street or else ensconced somewhere in the green heart of the land. She would not mutilate their personalities, and she would not lower herself to jibes over their appearances.

She would merely do to their flaws what the Herschels were doing to the distant stars and expose them in a merciless proximity. Lady Alicia would become a haughty betrayer of actual friendship, and Lady Marianne... Well, Lady Marianne would make a passable sister and accomplice to the villain of the piece.

The thoughts sent dark rivers of vengeful pleasure coursing through Lavinia's thoughts, making her body feel alive like a bird in the anticipation of a storm.

'Ladies.' A voice as cheerful as it was commanding rang out behind them. 'I hope you will forgive me for stealing your companion away.'

Lavinia would have known who it was even had she been born deaf and thus ignorant of his voice. The expressions of shock and then unease on the two women's features told her everything she needed to know.

Lord Hugh Granville, it seemed, was also in the mood for a public promenade. *I wonder why he is really here.*

Chapter 8

'I was surprised these two took you into their company,' Lord Granville said as they were taking a turn around the spa room, singularly indifferent to the fountain at the centre.

'I wouldn't quite name it so intimately.' Lavinia looked away as though she was very interested in the mock Roman tiles on the walls.

In one of the niches, a statue of an antique goddess stood, her translucent marble draperies clinging to her body. Lavinia's gaze lingered on her as she tried – and failed – to imagine appearing in public in such a garment as this even in the Mediterranean sun.

She imagined wearing something of the kind, not lace and feathers, the night Lord Granville confided in her on the balcony and then kissed her. Imagined the Roman silks falling down her shoulders, caressing her hips, thin as a nightgown and leaving even less to the imagination. Had Lord Granville touched her that night through something like that, she would have felt the heat of his fingers all the keener, and...

And that was why it was a blessing to the virtuous that the present fashion was very different from that of antiquity, Lavinia reminded herself.

'Have they been unkind to you?'

'Not at all.' It would have been hypocritical in the extreme on her part to first rebuff Lord Granville's advances and then enmesh him into the kinds of personal problems that usually only a husband, a father or a brother was to be called upon to deal with.

'Miss Dudley, you are a good novelist, but a good liar you are not.'

'No, I am speaking the truth,' she insisted. 'We've only had the briefest of exchanges anyway.'

'Have you? Because if you were, you wouldn't have been blinking quite so fast.'

Just how closely was this man watching her? There was something unnerving in the notion of Lord Hugh Granville – tall and lithe and quick-witted, a man with a sensual mouth, striking green eyes, and a string of conquests trailing after him like a lady's train – watching every twitch of her muscle.

Something unnerving, yes, but Lavinia would have been a liar to herself as well as to him if she did not acknowledge the idea also evoked an illicit thrill somewhere in the deep secret chambers of her flesh.

'I did not get a good night's sleep.' That was more or less the truth, anyway. 'That is all. How did your visit to the Peabodys go?'

'The aunt is not as vigilant as I feared. If she had a drop of your sense, she would have chased a courtier bearing gifts away with a broom.'

'She might have been hoping you wanted to court Miss Madeline in earnest,' Lavinia replied archly. 'Though in that case, she was indeed a fool.'

'The girl wasn't. I saw the eyes with which she regarded the bracelet. These were not the eyes of an innocence tempted. The creature is as cold as those diamonds and thinks herself worth that and more. I wouldn't waste your time trying to save her soul, Miss Dudley.'

'You've deduced all that on the strength of a single glance?' Lavinia raised her eyebrows.

'A man in my position needs to learn to discern meanings in glances whether he wants to or not.'

'A courtier, you mean?'

'A courtier most of all, but, honestly, any man deemed eligible. Otherwise, he is going to fall prey to the schemes of some pretty flower sooner rather than later and have his bones picked.'

'You are muddling your metaphors, your lordship. Flowers have no teeth.'

'There are jungle ones who do. They eat insects and the like. I've had a book of prints somewhere in Granville Hall.'

'Perhaps, you could send for it one day. I... I've always liked nature.'

'You would not have enjoyed an encounter with this piece of nature, I promise you. But maybe you will be able to see the book I am talking about if you are ever to visit me at Granville Hall with your husband.'

'Of course, yes.' Naturally, she was to have a husband one day even if Kurt von Wallmoden kept his word and helped her to accomplish her escape from the court without that. It was all well to scorn marriage as a pretty young woman, but should she persist with that attitude towards it for another decade, she would turn into a ridiculed spinster.

It would be like that walk with the sneering court ladies, only along a path that never ended. Lavinia was not sure what was a more dire fate – that or taking a husband she never wanted.

'What is your opinion of Miss Madeline?' she said briskly, just to turn the conversation onto a different path.

'I thought I've already given it?'

'Of her motives, yes. But I rather wonder what was your opinion of her as a woman.'

'You mean...whether I thought her alluring?'

'For example.'

'I cannot think of other examples that would have explained your words, to be honest. But if you want an answer... I thought the chit uncommonly pretty, yes. She has a kind of vivacity in her, underneath that proper exterior. Brains, too, which is always an asset.'

'Some rather think it a liability.'

'These men are fools, then. A wife without sense and intellect will not be a good companion or a good keeper of your estate, for that matter.'

'Neither you nor Kurt von Wallmoden would want Miss Madeline for a wife, though.'

'A mistress without sense and intellect will not be a good companion either.'

Lavinia wondered if the admiration for the other woman in Lord Granville's voice stemmed from something more serious than a passing glance. She wondered, too, if Kurt von Wallmoden grew tired of his paramour, Lord Granville might step in and acquire his mistress of sense and intellect.

Something clenched within her chest at the thought, the sensation making her want to look up and howl as though she was a wolf running wild and the pretty painted ceiling was the moon.

'What's wrong, Miss Dudley? You look stricken.'

When she did not reply, Lord Granville drew her into the shadow of one of the countless niches with their statues and their ornaments, clasped her shoulders, and looked into her eyes. 'Lavinia,' he said, and the sound of her Christian name on his lips seared her though as though he touched hot iron to her skin. 'What's wrong?'

'"'"'Nothing. Nothing.'

It was a lie, of course. Everything, quite everything, was wrong.

She wanted Hugh, the Viscount Granville who was not only a cold-hearted rake but a man with ambitions that shut any earnest intent towards a woman of low birth out. She might as well have wanted to devour the stars.

'I am worried about what is happening, your lordship.' Lavinia forced the words out. The court was a brutal school when it came to restrained manners. She had learnt well and therefore could now speak instead of screaming. 'That is all. That is the matter entirely.'

Chapter 9

The fact that Lavinia could now walk through the row of pews and the cold gazes of stained glass saints in the windows without flinching was certainly a testimony to something. She was not yet sure what, but it was definitely nothing good.

'Miss Dudley!'

Lavinia turned towards the familiar voice and saw Mrs Atwell with her jewel of a niece. Lavinia smiled at them. She had to. She was not going to exactly murder as she smiled, but, as far as she was concerned, her actions were about as irrevocable.

'It's a happy coincidence,' Madeline said, 'to see you like this. I don't think we've met after the assembly rooms.'

'I'm surprised we are meeting now,' Mrs Atwell added. 'I would have thought a woman of your position would prefer the chapel at the royal residence.'

She meant, of course, Lord Fauconberg's residence, temporarily touched with the royal grace and thus transfigured, like lead into gold.

There was a time Lavinia thought she was going to be similarly transformed by the great honour offered to her, by the new proximity to the royal radiance. That she was going to become more refined, more sophisticated, perhaps even more well-positioned to help her father's career and her own.

Three years later, the only thing she became was an emaciated creature shivering at every wrong sound. Lavinia wondered if there was some hidden flaw in her that made her wither where others bloomed.

'I've heard the local church has beautiful' – Lavinia cast her glance about surreptitiously – 'windows.'

'Lord Granville told us of your good fortune, Miss Dudley. That Her Majesty took mercy on you and took you to be her companion.'

'Hardly a mercy. I was not a street urchin when the word of *Miranda* came to her ears.'

'Oh, *Miranda* is all well and good,' Mrs Atwell replied airily. 'But no woman in the world has ever risen on the strength of her pen, has she?'

'Mary Wollstonecraft did.'

'Much good that it did her, the shameless creature! A daughter out of wedlock, a marriage to that malcontent... If she were my daughter – or, indeed, niece – I would have died of shame. You need not look so very peeved, Miss Dudley. Such a fate will never befall you. Coming to court was such a splendid opportunity for you. I imagine you have plenty of suitors there.'

Did she really look peeved? However much sympathy Lavinia felt for the poor Madeline – Lord Granville's insinuations about her character were certainly a courtier's cynicism – it did not mean she need to extend the same to her aunt.

'Not plenty,' Lavinia replied as gravely as though she were an earnest heroine of one of her own stories. 'But I do have one. Have you met the viscount of Granville?'

Madeline Peabody's expression was serene. She had no reason for jealousy, whether she believed Lavinia or not – she had her heart set on another. Mrs Atwell's expression, however, had to be seen to be believed.

'I believe we have been introduced,' she finally said, her pale grey eyes assessing Lavinia anew from her head crowned with a chip hat to the buckles on her shoes. 'In the assembly rooms.'

'He is a good man, isn't he?' Lavinia asked. The pretence was out-rageous, but she was having a surprising lot of mischievous fun with it.

'I formed the same opinion when he came to call on me and dear Madeline. He complimented her skill on the harpsichord very cour-teously. You are right, Miss Dudley, he is a very genteel kind of man.'

Something rose in Lavinia – something that had slept inside her, coiled and silent, for three years. 'I believe he told me about it. He did comment on Miss Madeline's becoming modesty. Such self-effacing manner. I believe it is your influence, Mrs Atwell.'

'I taught her everything I could,' she replied vaguely.

'Were I a different woman,' Lavinia continued, 'and you a different woman, too, I might have suspected you of having untoward ambi-tions. But I have heard of your virtues and Miss Madeline's, too. His lordship told me about in great detail. I know your position when it comes to such things.'

'I do expect you are knowledgeable indeed.'

This last pinprick, the hint at Lavinia being the dreaded thing that was a bluestocking, was left without a response. Instead, Lavinia ex-pressed a bland hope for a good sermon as a farewell and went to take her place in the pews. When she brushed her hand against that of the studiously silent 'Madeline, she tucked a small note into her palm. Her pale fingers closed around it eagerly.

When the champagne-like sensation of a brief victory won subsided, Lavinia felt more wicked than ever before. Helping a man ruin an unmarried woman while spewing concealed venom on the latter's guardian sounded like something the villainess from a novel might do, not the heroine. She was resolved to sit through the sermon with her eyes upon her hands.

'I, and wiser men than I, have often talked of the need for greater modesty in the female attire,' the vicar said, his voice as gentle as it was clear. 'But the choice of garments is not the only, not even close to being the greatest, one a young woman can make that will show her good sense and virtue. Much more important is one's choice of friends.'

Lavinia raised her gaze, startled. She recognised the topic. Not the precise words – these, of course, had been slightly altered and repurposed – but the direction...

'No person who possesses good sense himself,' he continued, 'would call for a young woman to be cut off from innocent delights of friendship and to be imprisoned in four walls, as is most sorrowfully the case in some popish countries.'

Yes, it was definitely something from Fordyce. The references to the cruelty of foreign Catholic patriarchs and the misery of their over-controlled female charges were definitely there in sermon number five.

'I am not of the number of men who claim that female friendship always has the sincerity of a viper in the grass. I do confess that most friendships between men I have seen in my life are steadier and somewhat more earnest than those I have observed between unmarried women, but that is not to say that better cases are unknown. But even in these cases, the vivacity of friendship can sometimes overflow into folly.

'It is as advisable for young woman to seek the friendship of the wise and the sedate as it is for them to stay away from novels of corrupting tendencies. There are plenty of tragedies I should not put into words where the gaiety of a young woman with more sensibility than sense has led her friend onto a path of vice.'

The sermon went on, turning later into a warning for the young ladies here. The vicar said firmly, 'Although the desire to please and accommodate men is a natural striving and even useful in the light of their future matrimony, it could lead to competition with bosom friends in question that rarely ends in anything good.'

Lavinia, however, barely paid attention to the vicar's warning, having already known what he would say. Her face felt as though flames were about to burst through her skin. Many years ago, she used to read Fordyce as a young girl in her father's library, delighting in his gentleness and charity and insistence upon the importance of the female sex. She had told herself back then, not in so many words, that she would one day lead such a life as to make the author proud were he to learn of it. She even envisaged meeting him one day and receiving his impressed praise. In her adolescent, half-formed mind, this imagined occasion had all the significance being crowned with laurels once held for Roman poets.

Lavinia had never imagined that one day she would find herself on the other side of his moral divide – the danger warned about in his sermons, the darkness behind the lines. The finely dressed false acquaintance, the one who would lead others astray.

If Lord Granville was a rake, she was a hypocrite for considering herself better. If he was a rake, they would make a fine couple.

No one would know of her involvement unless Madeline Peabody would decide to accuse her openly after the inevitable abandonment – perhaps one that would come years later but maybe only weeks later. But Lavinia would know. How on earth would she be able to look in people's eyes as they proclaimed the improving virtues of her novel and the novels to come? For that matter, how on earth would she be able to write them?

When she wrote *Miranda*, it was a joyful exercise of the ideas that had been growing out of her mind for a long time. When she wrote her tortured tragedies, it was a natural product of her emaciated soul. But thinking – doing – one thing and piously extolling another was beyond her abilities. She had always been made out of whole cloth.

There was only one thing to do. If she were to be consistent, she had to stop professing false virtue to the man she now knew she wanted with every fibre of her being.

Lavinia barely recalled the journey back to the tiny room found for her at Lord Fauconberg's residence. She barely even recalled looking for writing supplies or where she managed to find them – although the burning impatience that accompanied the search was memorable indeed.

When she finally had paper and ink and all the writing implements, she poured the letter upon the blank page as though the words came from some overflowing cauldron. It was a red-hot lava of a letter. She abandoned all chronology and pretence of measured arguments – for what arguments could possibly be needed here? She wrote of the revelation that came over her in the Cheltenham spa room among the almost bare statues and then of the wicked interest that flickered within her as early as the royal birthday ball.

She wrote of the savage frustration she felt at the mere notion that Hugh – she felt that a woman ready to forsake her virtue for a man was entitled to call him by his Christian name at least – could find any other woman alluring. She wrote of her jumbled, angry fantasies of him leading a lover through the palace corridors to sport with in his bedroom. She crowned it all with what, in that moment, seemed like good reasoning. Since she was likely to be dismissed from court shamefully when Queen Charlotte learnt of her new position as a lord's mistress, it would even, in a way, solve her problem.

It seemed almost neat, possessing a kind of perverse logic. Finally, Lavinia signed her name. Then, her hands trembling as one trembles from a chill or a fever, she stacked the sheets into a careful three-page construction. Since the postal service was never to see this letter, she did not have to apply any economizing tricks as she usually used in sending letters – turning the sheets horizontally and overwriting the existing text with perpendicular lines to save space, for instance. No, this was to be one of those letters passed from hand to hand and burnt in a fireplace after reading.

However, it was late spring, and it occurred to Lavinia that Hugh would have trouble convincing anyone that lighting the fireplace in his rooms was a normal course of action. Well, she supposed he would then have to shred the letter with his fingers until no one could discern the meaning of the pieces. Provided he had the patience for it, of course. Lavinia doubted he did. She might have been in a grip of shameful passion, but it did not precisely render her an idiot.

Her eyes fell upon one of the paragraphs on the first page. First drafts rarely came out clean, but this was an embarrassment even for a first draft. The comparison of love with flame was trite in the extreme, and the phrase that followed... Heavens, it made even her unfinished tragedies look like the lost works of the Bard. Or, at the very least, of Christopher Marlowe.

Lavinia recalled the evening concert and Hugh's incising criticism of their prose, delivered in a whisper. The last thing she wanted was to demonstrate even worse ineptitude in a letter that was to decide her fate. Lavinia reached for a clean sheet of paper and began the work anew.

When, several versions later, the sun was already ripening into sunset, Lavinia reread what appeared to be a satisfactory letter, and the dark storm in her chest calmed itself somewhat. She was guilty, her inner voice judged, and undeniably so, but would her ruin somehow mitigate Madeline Peabody's? Lavinia doubted that. She could do better things. She could dedicate the years ahead to instilling sense and virtue in her nieces, lady readers, and friends, to whom she vowed to be a better companion than she had been to Miss Madeline.

Although, had she really been a companion to Madeline Peabody? A chance acquaintance was, perhaps, a better choice of words. Would she have managed to talk her out of continuing this contact with the king's errant relative even if he could? Why would a young woman, especially if Hugh was right, and Miss Peabody had some ambition in her blood, pay any heed to the words of some chit she had seen a few times in her whole life as opposed to the glitter of a nobleman's promise?

Clearly, the most sensible course of action was to tear the letter up most thoroughly the way she hoped Hugh would do. But, sense or no, she had sunken hours of labour in this letter – as much as she ever spent on a chapter intended for an actual publication. Destroying the fruit of one's own work had never been particularly easy for anyone, even those who thought their writing a shameful secret or a fanciful hobby – and Lavinia belonged to neither group.

Perhaps, she thought, blackening out the names and places, one day it would make a fine chapter in truth. A part of a narrative she was going to invent one day when she was away from the court for good. Until then… She hesitated. Until then, it might be better if she carried it on her person. Even with the names blacked out, there was always a chance someone going through her things – a malicious lady, a curious maid, or Mrs Schwellenberg herself – would interpret it in the most scandalous way possible. Or, even if they did not believe it, they would pretend to.

Lavinia knew it now. She thought of Lady Alicia and her lovely, venomous friend. She thought, for that matter, of Hugh who had gained access to her room easily. Even with the dreams of dramatic ruin buried, she did not want to relinquish the use of his name, for surely it hurt no one when pronounced solely in her thoughts. She was far from the proper corridors of power and pomp, but that didn't mean she could trust everyone at court. She couldn't trust anyone anywhere.

Chapter 10

A few nights later, Lavinia awoke from the sound of powerful, urgent knocking on her door.

The queen was her first thought. She must have woken up in the middle of the night and needed her. The king was her second thought. Maybe he had another moment of wildness, illusions taking hold of his brain.

Lavinia opened the door, fully expecting to find Lady Alicia or her older comrade-in-arms on the other side of the doorstep. Instead, she saw Hugh standing there, breathing heavily, a piece of paper gripped in his left hand.

Lavinia's blood drained from her face. She wanted to open the chest of drawers and check if the pages of her ill-fated, unsent letter were still safely crumpled within the cloth. Could it – could someone – while she slept...

'Do you know why I am here?' Hugh asked breathlessly, filling out the doorway, tall and lithe, with his cravat slightly askew.

'Not because you wanted to wish me sweet dreams, I suspect.'

'No. Did you receive anything? From Miss Peabody?'

'Nothing. What did she—'

'In lieu of an answer, he thrust the hand holding the note towards her and offered her the piece of paper. Lavinia read the first few lines quickly, and her blood grew cold. 'Why did she write to you?'

'I suppose she wanted to share her good fortune with me.'

'But why not myself? I mean... I wanted to—"

'Because she wanted to impress me and considered you a nonentity not worth impressing,' Hugh said flatly. 'Which does not improve my opinion of Miss Peabody one bit.'

'''Was that true? Could the woman Lavinia's imagination had already cast in the form of a ruined innocent really have been such a calculating chit? The letter in Hugh's hand spoke of it far louder than Hugh's own impressions could have. Madeline Peabody was careless with her written words as much as she had once been careful with her spoken ones. Perhaps, a lifetime of careful silence had been finally broken. 'Give me a moment to read the entire letter,' Lavinia said, and Hugh nodded.

I am writing to you to thank you for your tremendous help in reuniting me with the man in whom I had placed all my yearnings for years, rejecting every other suitor. When you receive it, I am likely to already be married and related by marriage, however distantly, to the family tree of our own gracious sovereign. There are no words on my tongue to express how conscious I am of this high honour. Please be sure that my house shall ever be open to you and that my husband and I are going to consider you a dear friend.

With the greatest regard,

Magdalena von Wallmoden

Magdalena! Lavinia shook her head. *She does seem eager to please.* She could imagine how ardently she seized upon her German lessons, when she had first met this son of a bastard. She handed the letter back to Hugh.

'She is a fool,' Hugh said sharply.

'An ambitious fool.'

'Ambition doesn't always bring with it good brains.'

'Doesn't she know...'

'I don't imagine her paramour made a point to tell her.'

'The Royal Marriages Act.' Lavinia exhaled loudly. 'Heavens, even I know this one. There are still endless papers proclaiming His Majesty a tyrant for signing it.'

'Miss Peabody, or whatever she is now, doesn't strike me as the kind of woman who reads opinionated papers.'

'She is still Miss Peabody. Just a ruined Miss Peabody.'

That, after all, was the whole point. The Royal Marriages Act, signed two decades before, stipulated that no descendant of George II could marry without the sovereign's consent. If he or she did, the sovereign in question could easily proclaim the marriage invalid.

Kurt von Wallmoden, the son of a bastard though he was, was the son of a royal bastard. The second he tried to present Madeline to his crowned relative, everything would change. Kurt would most likely only be banished from court for a time. Madeline, though, her marriage proclaimed illegitimate, would be regarded as von Wallmoden's mistress. And that was if the speakers would choose their words carefully and gently. Which Lavinia doubted they would.

'We need to stop her.' Lavinia raised her head. 'Stop them.'

'Do you truly care for her so?'

'When I gave von Wallmoden that promise, I knew another woman's ruin would be the outcome. I loathed myself for agreeing, but I thought I had no choice. Well, I have a choice now. I soothed myself with telling myself it's within her power of will not to succumb, and I won't pretend it's a good excuse for me, but at least – at least it was some excuse. But now – if he wants to get her in his bed by deception... I can no longer pretend I have even *that* excuse.'

'God Almighty,' Hugh murmured, looking at her with a strange, crystalline fascination. 'You are a lady of byzantine complexity, aren't you? Or, at least, the thoughts going on inside that fair head are labyrinthine enough.'

'My head isn't all that fair,' Lavinia replied in an automatic urge to dampen any compliment down, to grey herself out of the landscape. 'Do you have any idea of where they could have gone? Besides the Scottish border, which, let us face it, is a bit too far from here for Miss Peabody to assume you wouldn't have read the letter before they reached it?'

'A royal relative would have little trouble procuring a wedding license discreetly though some expense would be required. No need for the Scottish border. Prestbury is more likely. It's the closest place with a good parish church.'

'There I must go then.'

'Alone? I cannot allow that.'

'Whyever not? I am not as fragile as I seem.' How could she explain to him, make him understand, that it was the four walls of Windsor Castle, of her own closet of a room, of the endless ceremonies and endless jibes, that made her as weak as the victim of some blood-drinking monster of legend? Even here, in Cheltenham, when the bonds constraining her loosened but a thumb, Lavinia discovered she still could breathe – breaths rapid and shallow but breaths nonetheless.

A wistful thought entered her head. Perhaps, if he had known her as she was in her father's house, he could have loved her. But, of course, had she remained in her father's house, he would have never met her in the first place.

''No. Because these roads aren't safe. Because it's raining. Because the horse could slip in the mud. Because a highwayman could hold a lone woman up and make her pray to the high Heavens that he will only have designs on her money.' Hugh stepped forward and did something unthinkable.

'He took Lavinia's face into his hands and looked into her eyes. 'I cannot allow you to put yourself in danger,' he added, his voice as soft as if he were whispering to a mare.

'Because we are co-conspirators?'

'Because…' Hugh paused. 'Because I have a reason to want to prevent this scandal, too. When it becomes known, who do you think Miss Peabody's aunt will remember as hovering around her virtuous niece weeks before her fall?'

'I'll likely take the brunt of it.'

'Well, I don't want you to take the brunt of it!' he all but snarled, the ferocity unlike anything she had heard from him before.

'Why?' Lavinia whispered. She could see her own shadowy reflection in his green eyes. Here, in the night, it was not the merry green of the forest but something darker, infinitely wilder.

'I've already told you once.' He released her face. 'I might be a rake, but a finished scoundrel I am not.'

Chapter 11

 he first thing Hugh heard when he and Lavinia opened the door to the room upstairs was Madeline Peabody's merry voice. 'You are too late.'

''She was sitting upon the bed, her shining Sunday dress only lightly touched with rain. She must have come here in a good carriage arranged by her lover. She couldn't have been a greater contrast with Lavinia, whose riding habit was clinging to her body, heavy with water, and whose hair was soaked despite the hood.

Hugh knew which woman he would have rather been looking upon.

It was not difficult to find the small town in the vicinity of Cheltenham. He used to ride all over these lands in his carefree adolescence, and the names of them were as familiar and sweet on his tongue as crispy green apples.

Had he been alone, he would have reached Prestbury hours before and already scoured the inns. But he was not alone, and Miss Dudley was not used to riding. There was nothing in her earlier life to prepare her even for stately riding along Rotten Row, let alone a madcap dash through the night rain. He had to keep to her side, his fingers light upon the reins. The image of Lavinia losing her balance and slipping out of her saddle right upon the hard ground was simply refusing to leave the inner chambers of his mind.

But she had kept her balance well – kept her posture, even. Kept her lips closed. Kept herself from any complaint.

Kurt von Wallmoden was sitting at the modest desk in the corner of the room. By the looks of it, he was writing a letter.

'We aren't,' Hugh said briefly. 'Von Wallmoden, we need to talk.'

'I hope you aren't asking me to send my delightful bride out of the room?' The nobleman stood up. 'After all, in that case, we would need to put your own lady friend outside the door, and I don't think you would do that.'

'I know about your plan.'

'Do you indeed.'

'It wasn't a very complicated one,' Hugh said venomously.

'Such indignation from our...resident saint, isn't it? A man who has never had a weakness for the female sex?'

'I did.' He used to before Lavinia Dudley filled his thoughts, and that one was no weakness but a disease that invaded one's very bones. 'But, fortunately, they also had a weakness for me. I never had the need to deceive them with sham marriages to get them into bed.'

He knew he was being crude, and he felt Lavinia stiffen beside him. The sensation gave him a reckless, perverse determination. Let her remember what he was and recoil. Perhaps then, the shocked tenderness that he saw in her eyes when he took her face into his hands would wither and tease him with no false hopes anymore.

'The marriage is very much real,' Madeline Peabody piped up.

Kurt von Wallmoden nodded, laying a hand upon her shoulder.

'It is real,' he said simply. 'And my royal relative is going to have to recognise it.'

'He isn't, and he won't.'

The older man nodded at the papers he left upon the desk.

'Do you know what these are?' he asked. 'Letters describing His Majesty's current condition in exquisite detail. The papers are going to be rather interested to find out the truth about his latest antics. It would rather shatter the image he and you and the other equerries and countless servants worked so hard to create, won't it? It would certainly make it rather difficult to pretend that the emperor has any clothes on afterwards.'

'Von Wallmoden, we are at war. The people need to be a united front. They need something to believe in. That was the whole purpose of coming to Cheltenham. Not so much inspecting the new local militia, definitely not enjoying the healing waters. It was to show the subjects a parade of glittering symbols. Like those effigies of saints they carry around in Catholic countries on feast days.'

'I know that, Granville. So would His Majesty, and the prime minister, and every last man or woman on the palace staff. The need to keep King George's true condition secret would overwhelm any resistance. Precisely because, as you say, the people need something to believe in.'

'I know a better way. Take Miss Peabody—'

'Address her correctly as Gräfin von Wallmoden.'

'Take your radiant bride with you to your father's court in Germany. There, you would have a better chance of keeping your marriage only a minor scandal and not the sort that would involve the royal family. His Majesty might overlook it if you are to keep as far from Windsor Castle as possible.'

'Now, why on earth would I do that?'

'Because there might be some shred of honour in you. You are man of fine blood. Prove it.'

'Since when do you care about anyone's honour but that of your own dead father, Granville? Ah.' Kurt von Wallmoden smiled a twisted smile, his gaze shifting to Lavinia, who was standing there wet to the last thread. 'I think I see. Now you have a living reason to pretend at integrity and caution, don't you?'

'I have not the slightest idea what are you talking about.'

'I think you do. I think you are a hypocrite of the first water, Granville. Haranguing me for marrying a genteel young lady while you yourself are throwing yourself at the feet of a tutor's get. I wonder what it is that you saw in her. She is as cold as a stone statue. When she finally falls into your bed, your extremities are going to freeze off.'

''A white-hot, blind rage flooded Hugh's mind. In one swift action, an arrow in righteous flight, he took off his glove and tossed it at Kurt von Wallmoden's feet. 'I have an offer for you,' Hugh said, his anger glacial in his voice. There was no usual desire to persuade in him, no honeyed charm left. The only words in his throat were those of action. 'I am challenging you to a duel, von Wallmoden. You have insulted a lady who deserved none of it and dragged her into a sordid scheme she lost much more tears over than either you or Miss Peabody have. If you are to lose and survive, you are going to take your – wife – into exile to the Continent, and you are going to never let Miss Dudley's name cross your lips on either side of the Channel.'

'Fine words for a man with all the confidence and skills of a pup. What if it is you who is going to be beaten, Granville?'

'Then you are going to be free to throw all caution to the wind and take your bride to the royal court when it returns to Windsor.'

''Kurt von Wallmoden was a tall, dark presence, towering too high for this puny room – or he tried to be so. 'And what is going to happen should I put a bullet through your head, Granville?'

'In that case, you would have to leave the country anyway. So, in a way, I would have won.'

'How noble of you. Dying for a lady's honour. I would have almost believed you, had I not heard of your exploits for years. There is not a harlot in the towns of Cotswolds you hadn't sampled, not a married lady at court you hadn't enjoyed. You didn't give a pig's foot about their honour. So why this one?'

'Because she is a lady of great virtues. I am not talking about the fretting of never being completely alone with a gentleman without matronly witnesses. I mean real virtues. I also mean passions that no rote learning could drain out of her completely, and that is a rare treasure in our age of walking paper dolls and papier-mâché cavaliers. I mean a talent that is never neglected and strength in the face of mistreatment grown men would have long since exploded under.'

Hugh felt Lavinia's keen, anxious eyes upon him. Hugh and his opponent knew it was not Madeline – Madeline, who was sitting through the crude and angry talk with the face of a patient saint, suffering for a future bliss – they were talking about.

Hugh wondered if Lavinia, too, knew. He also wondered if she would care, after von Wallmoden's revelations, about his confirmation of what Lavinia had long suspected from the rumours. His prim and proper Lavinia, the mirror and the light of womanhood.

Suddenly, it felt easy to walk into the rain on a cold spring dawn and point a gun at another man's chest. Or even to have one pointed at his own person. He smiled.

'Sharp nails dug into his arm, and Lavinia whispered, her voice ferocious, 'Don't you dare.'

It was the passion for words that betrayed her. The clinging obsession with words, as though those sounds or signs on a paper were to her what gin was to the unforunates of St Giles.

If not for that passion, that obsession, she would not have been struck so completely dumb with Hugh's speech, forgetting, for a second, the doomed decision he was taking at the moment.

He said she – for only a complete ninnyhammer would not have been able to understand his misdirection, his evasive lack of names – was a lady of great virtues, and passion, and talent, and strength.

The revelation was so blinding it had taken her a second to come to her senses and grasp his arm as though she were a jealous wife. Lavinia didn't loosen her grasp even when Hugh stiffened.

'''This is not your quarrel,' Hugh said sharply. In the candlelit murk of the room, his face was paler than usual and so lined with shadows as though he had already lived the remaining decades of his life.

'You are starting it in my name. Therefore, it is my quarrel.'

'If Lord Granville was to withdraw the challenge so suddenly, without the other side having apologized for the insult,' Kurt von Wallmoden explained, 'he is to behave like a coward. Surely you are not going to demand that a man clearly dear to you behaves like a coward, Miss Dudley?'

'This is ridiculous.'

'This is the way of men of noble blood. I understand if your father has never imparted it to you. After all, there was to be no application of such knowledge in the life he thought you would lead.'

'Then apologize,' Lavinia demanded. She was done with pretty pleading. 'Apologize, and take Madeline to the Continent.'

'You seem to think Madeline as a kind of doll to be hauled around at will. I suppose desire for a better life is far from the mind of a woman as virtuous as you, but my wife wants to take her place at my relative's court as much as I want her to do so.'

'Madeline,' Lavinia addressed the redhead, who was sitting sensibly motionless. 'This is madness. You cannot wish for this. Do you understand that a duel can well end in death?'

Madeline Peabody – now apparently Magdalena von Wallmoden – turned her pretty head towards her, and Lavinia saw such utter disdain in her eyes that it would have withered her on the spot had it been a true venom.

'You simpering creature,' she said. 'You goody two-shoes. I wonder if there is a living fibre in your body or if it is all porcelain in your flesh and water in your veins. Oh yes, Miss Dudley, I understand how a duel can end in death. Except it won't be my husband's. He is excellent with a rapier.'

'Duels are usually fought with pistols—"

'In our country, perhaps. Not in the German states. Kurt was the one challenged, so he has the right to choose the weapon. I hope Lord Granville paid some attention with his fencing tutor. This way, he might survive for ten minutes instead of five.'

'Madeline, you cannot want this.'

'I very much know what I want. Do you think it was easy to live with my brooding hen of an aunt, pretend to be a creature straight out of conduct handbooks for young ladies? I seethed every single moment.

Sometimes, during these long sermons, I felt like if I cut my palm the blood that would flow out of it would be pure flame and burn the whole edifice down.'

Lavinia had heard enough. In the back of her mind, she filed the pretty speech away for a future use in some distant novel, but here and now, she still had had enough. She grasped the sitting woman by the arm, pulled her from the bed, and marched her out of the room, none too gently. She screeched and fought; she was not the only one whose blood finally caught fire.

Lavinia slammed the door. She was now alone in the corridor with one very irate redhead.

'No arguments left, I see?' the latter asked archly, her cheeks flaming. 'You are now resorting to manhandling?'

'Listen to me, you – you ninnyhammer. I see you are imagining yourself Lady Macbeth, but in reality, you are an utter fool. You've heard it right that King George is rarely lucid now. Who do you suppose it will fall to, to make decisions about arrangements at court?'

'His eldest son, of course. There are talks of him becoming regent any day now, and he has an appreciation for brave men and lovely women to decorate his court. Cheltenham is not the backwater you think us to be. We hear things.'

'Clearly not very well, because the Regency Bill isn't likely to be signed any time soon. There was a talk of it some years ago, but the notion is dead and buried now.' It felt as though a true, living fire was erupting from her every pore. All the burning she had stifled for the last few years and, in some ways, since her proper, Fordyce-reading childhood. 'The person who guides the life of the court is Queen Charlotte. Unlike her husband, she is thinking very clearly indeed.'

'Her Majesty is a woman with most women's soft heart. I know how to elicit sympathy from women.' It was as if the hands of an invisible sculptor had touched the pale wax of Madeline's face. A second ago, it was a mask of contempt; now, it took on the tenderest vision of humility one could possibly imagine.

If Madeline Peabody was not quite so respectably born and was not setting her sights quite so high, perhaps she should have taken to the stage. She would have made Sarah Siddons anxious and thrown Mr Sheridan into raptures.

'Her Majesty? A soft heart? I would have never thought to hear these words in one sentence. Do you think her daughters call their abode a nunnery for the quality of singing?'

'Princesses of all kinds have always been sheltered.'

'Have queens always...' Lavinia paused. An idea had dawned, a memory. A warm spring evening, a chilling tale, snatches of golden laughter from the rooms at her back. 'Have queens always ended their days in captivity, too?'

'"What on earth are you talking about?'

'Have you never heard the tragedy of Queen Caroline Mathilde? No, I imagine it is not the tale your husband would tell you. It might have put you off accepting his generous offer, after all.'

'Quit speaking in riddles, Miss Dudley.'

'If you want. She was King George's own sister, married to the monarch of Denmark. She scandalized her brother by taking a lover.' Lavinia left out the queen's obvious, glaring misbehaviour of capturing the kingdom's power for herself and the lover in question. If she didn't, Madeline might have reasonably pointed out treason was a far greater offense than any elopement, any secret marriage. Lavinia didn't want that. Words had power, and their absence did, too.

'What do I care?'

'Let me finish, please. When the favourite was cast down, Queen Caroline Mathilde was initially supposed to have been sent back to

England into an honourable exile. She never reached these shores. Her Majesty was against it. She would suffer no wanton, scandalous women at her court. Her husband was the king, but her word was law. Queen Caroline Mathilde was a sister to one king, and a wife to another, and a mother to one future monarch, too, but that didn't save her. Her Majesty wanted her punished, so punished she was. She died before reaching thirty years of age in a dismal fortress in Germany. She was, by all accounts, beautiful.' Lavinia had never been a cruel creature, but she could not help but add, 'Just like you.'

'How do I know you are even telling the truth?' Madeline asked, but the ferocious resolve in her voice had waned.

'You can ask your husband.'

'Kurt!' Madeline pushed the door open, running back into the room like a redheaded hurricane, all pretence of composure gone. 'Did it truly happen as Miss Dudley tells?'

'Did what happen?'

'The king's sister. Did she truly end her life in exile thanks to Queen Charlotte's disapproval of her ways?'

'Oh, that old story?' Kurt von Wallmoden waved his hand dismissively. 'I suppose you could say that. But that's never going to happen to you, if this is what you fear. Queen Caroline Mathilde had a royal honour to uphold and failed while you... Well, you have not a drop of royal blood in your veins.'

'Yes. That's the problem,' Madeline replied angrily. 'If a queen could die in captivity because she was not virtuous enough for Her Majesty's ways, what hopes do I have? I could just... I could just – disappear.'

'Her Majesty isn't bloodthirsty,' Hugh remarked, his face as bland as though he were playing vingt-et-un with his friends. 'At worst, she would simply arrange for you to be married off somewhere nice and distant as soon as this unfortunate union is proclaimed invalid.'

Madeline grew pale. Not in the decorous, cream-white way tragic heroines on history paintings did but with the pallor of desperation and bone. 'I don't want this,' she uttered, her tone an admirable – but not quite successful – attempt at steadiness. 'A guillotine, but not this.'

'You have a talent for melodrama,' Hugh observed. These was a hint of cruelty in his voice. Could it have been thanks to the words she hurled at Lavinia? 'No one is going to cut your head off. You are going to live and grow old as a respectable, plain-bonneted wife somewhere in the far reaches of Northumberland. Your husband, whoever he will be, is going to expect some gratitude for accepting the leavings of a scandal, but I expect you know that already. You are, after all, so very worldly, so very knowledgeable, if your speech in Miss Dudley's direction is to be believed.'

'I will not grow old as a respectable wife of—'

'A strange choice, given the alternative.' All Hugh's charm, all his sleek magnificence, had now turned into a sharpened steel. 'Would you prefer to die young, then?'

'You are talking to my wife, Granville,' Kurt von Wallmoden growled. 'Not to one of the Cyprians you are no doubt more accustomed to.'

'Me? Accustomed to Cyprians? Never. It might be a strange notion to you, but I prefer women who are eager and willing for my own person. Letting one's wealth do the seduction is the path of a coward.'

'Kurt,' Madeline whispered urgently, looking up at her husband. 'Don't let this man rattle you.'

'He insulted my wife. He all but compared you to a lady of the frail sisterhood—"

'Let him compare me to the breakfast kippers, if he so wishes. I want to live and to be with you.'

'"Of course. He is your only hope of advancement, after all,' Hugh said, stating the obvious.

'Please,' Madeline pleaded as though not hearing him. 'Perhaps, we really should go to the Continent. Your father, your brothers – they are not going to annul our marriage, are they? There were stranger unions you've told me...'

'Of course, they won't. They would lack the legal mechanisms to do that.' Lavinia felt entirely calm, as if standing in the centre of a great storm. 'Of course, they might petition His Majesty to do so on their behalf...but there is smaller chance of that than of Queen Charlotte doing so.'

Lavinia thought of Queen Charlotte – the resplendent figure in the royal chapel, murmuring disapproval at the appearance of Dr Johnson's friend married to a foreigner; the pale woman in bed, keeping her composure and supporting her husband's delusion as though she were putting on one of those royal masques the courts of the last century were so famed for; the iron-willed mother, determined to keep her daughters about her even if it meant depriving them of love and marriage and motherhood themselves.

The keeper of traditions, who possibly was the sole person within the palace walls – not counting, of course, her royal husband – who took the sermons of her childhood exactly at their word and spent decades trying to wrestle her world into conforming to those moral tenets. If her sister-in-law led a life bloodier and more lascivious than those tenets allowed – so much the worse for the sister-in-law, queen or no.

And if a no-name young woman from a small town did the same, or nearly, in Her Majesty's mind, the same – so much the worse for the young woman.

'You were keener than me to be introduced at the court at Windsor,' Kurt von Wallmoden told his bride. 'You were burning to be acknowledged as my wife.'

'I am burning still. But what use would it be to be introduced as your wife one moment only to be repudiated the next and ruined in the bargain?'

'You won't be ruined.'

'You could have told me,' she whispered, her lips set not in petulance but in a kind of harshness that suggested she would not forget this diet of false hopes. 'You could have told me of the Royal Marriages Act.'

'King George isn't going to invoke it. Not with the sword I am holding over his reputation's neck.'

'Would his wife not invoke it either?' Madeline asked pointedly. 'She might decide our marriage is a greater shame than a little scandal in the papers.'

'She won't.' Kurt von Wallmoden's voice was full of the utter conviction of someone who strode through life with an iron certainly of all one's efforts being successful and all one's enemies falling away unopposed.

'But she might.' Madeline looked up into his eyes. 'She might, Kurt. What is going to happen to us then? What is going to happen to me?'

'Swear upon whatever you hold sacred that, if I take you to the Continent, you are not going to spend your years pining for the glories you've almost had and blaming me for losing them. Swear it, Madeline, and we will leave for Dover tomorrow morning.'

Madeline stood in the middle of the room, distraught and lovely in the candlelight.

Lavinia held her breath. She had long since stopped feeling pain from the fingernails she was pressing into her palms; her skin had become numb to physical sensations. Some of it was the cold. Most of it was the mute terror, the mute bravery, and the storm surrounding her calm.

Hugh was looking on, alert and brave, his eyes clear as the green glass of some old vessel. His sweet mask, his pretty languor – he had lost them somewhere on this journey to the godforsaken inn, and they were not in any hurry to gather themselves from the shards.

'I swear,' Madeline, now Magdalena von Wallmoden, claimed, pressing a hand to the spot on her chest where her heart was most likely beating, 'Upon my reputation as a good woman.'

Chapter 12

'So, what are we to do now?' Hugh asked when the door closed behind them after what felt like eternity. They were left standing in the corridor among the sleepy rooms.

'Talk to the innkeeper about two rooms on the opposite ends of the corridor,' she said. 'And make sure we can count on his good testimony that we indeed took separate ones.'

'I doubt that people whose judgement you most fear would bother themselves with a good testimony of an innkeeper. They would hear that we disappeared together, that we were seen together at an inn, and that some noted that we went up together. That would be enough even for the milder of gossips...and I am not sure mild gossips exist at this court.'

At this court. The glittering fever dream of Windsor Castle, the ball at St James, and the morning ceremony of dressing Her Majesty had fallen so far into the back of Lavinia's mind over the course of this mad dash of a night that forcing them all back into recall felt almost unnatural.

With recollection came not so much fear but a kind of dull registration of a fact. Yes, she was likely to be exiled from court when the events of tonight came to light, especially since they would have to conceal their primary reason for the journey. If it were to be known they found a royal relative in the midst of conducting an unsuitable union and didn't drag him back by hook or by crook, being merely released from her duties would become, to Lavinia, a blessing.

She was likely to end up a shunned spinster once the news of the reason for her exile back to her family home crossed their little circle. All those plans. All those little schemes. Find a husband, then entrap a maiden, then prevent a mésalliance. And that was what they all came to.

'I suppose you are right.' Lavinia felt numb, and spent, and dejected. But, above it all, she felt tired.

'I have a plan to prevent that.' Hugh Granville stepped towards her.

'Another plan?' She smiled with only the corners of her mouth. 'Your plans so far have led me to a certain ruin. I wonder if the next one is going to end up with me being dead.'

'I don't think so. Unless we are to kill each other in marital quarrel.'

'In...' She stared at him, dumbfounded. Surely Viscount Granville couldn't have possibly meant...

'In a marital quarrel,' Hugh repeated, looking intently upon her as if trying to drink in the very outlines of her mouth. 'Of which, I suspect, we are to have many. If you accept my proposal.'

Her head became very light as if Madeline was right and her blood had truly turned to water.

'You cannot truly intend this.'

'I can. Moreover, which is more important, I do.'

'You are the heir to an ancient title.'

'Not that ancient. It has only been turned into a proper title by Henry VI, and my family received it even later from the Stuarts.'

'This is not what I meant! God Almighty, but you are impossible—''

'See, we are going to have marvellous marital quarrels, Lavinia. May I call you this? May I call you Lavinia? Even if you reject my proposal, do leave me at least this prize. Please.'

He was pleading with her. Viscount Granville, her rakish saviour, the man in whom passion and duty tangled together in such an impossible knot... was pleading with her. And it occurred to Lavinia that, perhaps, some knots were truly best sliced with swords sharp as vengeance.

'I know the abyss between us,' he continued. 'I am not the fool some think me to be. But it seems to me that this abyss is yawning much wider in your head than it does here in the world of things. It's those people – the first keeper of the robes, the ladies-in-waiting who wait for nothing but an opportunity to sink their claws into someone's flesh, Her Majesty with her prudery and her nunnery – they made you feel like you were mud on their slippers. You aren't. What you truly are... Well, I've already told that to Kurt von Wallmoden and trust you have a good memory. I would honestly never repeat anything said in his presence. The less I call the man to mind, the better.'

'I...' Lavinia opened her hands to him, palms upwards, not so much offering a touch as yearning for it. Then she remembered something. She opened her reticule and withdrew a letter of several pages folded in two. 'I wrote it when I was in a strange and dark mood,' she said, offering it to him.

''He was putting his heart on a platter for her. The least she could do was to respond in kind. Let him know that, in a moment of despair, she was ready to allow herself to be debauched.

'The names are inked out,' Hugh noted, his green gaze running over the first few paragraphs.

'I wanted to be sure no one would connect it to us if anyone...found it in my room.'

'Why did you keep it, then?'

'Because I thought to use it in some future novel,' Lavinia explained as though it were the most natural thing in the world.

'God,' Hugh said, looking at her, 'you are quite unlike anyone else in the world, aren't you?'

Lavinia swallowed. She wanted to bottle this gaze up like wine to store forever before it faded once he realised what she was offering him. It did fade. It was not replaced with a frown or anything else as obvious, but she noticed the whiteness that crept into Hugh's knuckles as he held the miserable pages.

'You were thinking to become my mistress?' he asked, raising his head.

'Lavinia's first instinct was to lower her eyes, to keep her silence, but there would have been no sense in that and no use. 'I thought it to be a better course. An honest course. I was... I thought I was...conniving in the ruin of another woman, and guarding my own virtue as a precious treasure at the same time seemed hypocrisy of the first water.'

'Your opinion of me must've been worse than I suspected if you thought I would agree to become your sacrificial altar.'

'You did kiss me on the balcony. I thought you found some allure in me.'

'I did. God help me, I do.'

'Even now, after I've shown you this?'

'After you've shown me you are a creature of labyrinthine logic and motives of some medieval saint? I can see how these could be detractions. But I'll do my best to untangle the former and teach you better than the latter.'

Him, teach her! The presumptuousness of it. Lavinia imagined just what he could teach her behind the closed door of a bedchamber when they would be undisturbed as a married couple should be. She imagined all the instruction his tireless capacity for mischief could provide her.

She blushed at the mental image, feeling her skin becoming strangely taut just as it did that night on the balcony.

'That is,' Hugh continued, 'if you will agree to become my wife. My Viscountess Granville.'

'I would,' Lavinia replied, her voice unsteady even to her own ears. 'I would. Only—'

'He clasped her around her waist, letting the unsent letter flutter to the ground, and drew her into a hungry kiss. The sensual power of it scattered her thoughts. Pressed close to his lithe, lightly muscular body, she felt the heat of his skin through the layers of clothing, burning as hotly as though she were pressed against him without a shirt between the two.

The notion fired her imagination up, and she thought of how it could truly be to be pressed against the man she loved with nothing to shield their skin from each other's.

Oh yes, the man she loved. She could now utter the dangerous word in her thoughts, for she was now going to be his wife. His. Lavinia's heart was beating hotly by the time the tight circle of his arms relaxed a little, allowing her to draw back.

'Only?' Hugh asked almost innocently as though there had been no interruption to the conversation.

Lavinia smiled. 'Only,' she said, 'we are still to get separate rooms here.'

'My little minx. You are going to tease me to distraction, aren't you?' he asked fondly.

'Have I ever teased you?'

'Oh, yes.'

'I would have thought my dress and conduct were very modest.'

'Not always. For example, ever since that evening at the theatre, I couldn't stop thinking about your dear ankles.'

'When I wore that green gown?'

'I would have lied,' Hugh said, his hands still upon her waist and his thumb stroking it warmly just as she had once imagined him to do, 'if I said I remembered the colour of the gown.'

Hugh Granville knew they did not have much time. Kurt von Wallmoden's disappearance would be known soon enough, and then the royal couple – or, rather, its female half – was going to be too preoccupied to listen to any petitions.

Therefore, when he rode back into Cheltenham on the coming morning, his bride by his side, he made straight for Fauconberg Lodge. He couldn't quite stop throwing glances at her as though there was a chance of her falling from her horse or some other disaster coming to her.

Rationally, he knew the notion was preposterous. On his less rational side, he felt apt to take on the whole world in order to shield her from more pain than Lavinia had already encountered on her path. If the pain in question could come from something as mundane as the hardness of spring ground, so be it, and he would take it up with nature.

'Are you nervous?' Lavinia whispered as they dismounted by Fauconberg Lodge.

It sounded sweetly similar, it occurred to Hugh, to what a newly wedded bride might say to her groom in anticipation of the wedding night. The notion made him regret the endless days and nights of empty beds that were going to stretch like a desert between the present moment and the moment he could finally claim her as his wife in every way. But now was not the time to think of the delights they could enjoy together. Now was the time to screw his courage to the sticking place.

'Of what?' Hugh asked, rather disingenuously. No man, least of all the viscount of Granville, would have liked to let his intended see he was indeed uneasy about confronting one of the most powerful women in the world – a woman who sent a queen to exile and cold death.

Lavinia seemed to have felt something unnamed beneath his bravado, for she squeezed his hand – as much in support as in her own search for it.

He had kissed her before, twice, and felt her respond, too. But, for some reason, it was this touch, offered by her boldly in broad daylight, that felt like a shift of the unseen plates of Earth.

'I'll make a maenad out of you yet,' he whispered in her ear and enjoyed the sight of her blush. He could have wagered Granville Hall on the fact her blush was not all anger.

When they went in, they were met with a sight now familiar– a gaggle of town worthies standing in the corridor leading to the stately home's drawing room, eager to see Her Majesty. It was like a familiar court tableau – courtiers, bored to the last wit, waiting for the door to

the royal apartments to open and for their audience to commence –
replicated in a provincial miniature.

There was a time Hugh took such situations with a dead seriousness
he rarely reserved for anything else. It was, after all, the milieu in which
his father's life had passed, in which his fortune has been made. Now,
the sheer pettiness and the ridiculousness of everything all but made
him laugh.

They didn't have to wait for long. A dark-haired lady-in-waiting
stepped through the doorway, no doubt shivering with disgust at the
petty surroundings in which she now had to uphold the majesty of the
ceremonies and went pale. Lady Alicia's eyes went to Lavinia.

It was clearly only the decades-bred habit of politesse that prevented her from running back into the room shouting about the errant
second 'keeper's arrival. She was visibly trembling with anticipation as
she motioned silently for Lavinia to step into the room before everyone else. Lady Alicia clearly thought Lavinia no longer merited any
courtesy, given her incorrect assumption of Lavinia's current status.
Hugh wondered if her attitude would change once she was disabused
of the notion.

The drawing room of Fauconberg Lodge was a squalid affair even
compared to its equivalent in Granville Hall, let alone the throne room
in Windsor or St James. Had they been admitted to one of these
resplendent chambers, cold with marble and dripping with gilding,
the pair would have likely been humbled in spirit as was intended.
Here, now, however, seeing Queen Charlotte – in her pannier gown
and silver-white wig in the manner of the last decade with her retinue
– holding court from an armchair was comical rather than anything
else. It was a magnificent armchair made of giltwood but an armchair
nonetheless.

'Miss Dudley,' she said, her voice icy, her eyes trained like an archer's arrow upon his betrothed, who sank into a deep curtsy. 'I have expected you this morning.'

'I beg your forgiveness, Your Majesty,' Lavinia murmured. 'I can explain…'

'I doubt any explanation would be sufficient.'

No regal wrath here. No accusations of debauchery. She simply berated Lavinia as if she were a lazy housemaid who had forgotten to attend to her duties.

And no one was going to berate his Lavinia as if she were a lazy housemaid. Not the queen of Great Britain, not the queen of Sheba, not the queen of heaven.

'Your Majesty,' Hugh said. 'I am afraid it is me who deserves your anger here. It was my fault that Miss Dudley didn't reach you this morning, for I waylaid her with a singular request.'

'Have you indeed, Lord Granville?'

'I have, Your Majesty. My request was for Miss Dudley to become my wife. I am very happy to say that she has agreed to fulfil it.'

It was as though he stabbed someone, not proclaimed his intention to marry, judging by the way the room froze around him. Lady Alicia was looking at him with shock. Lady Marianne, standing in the corner, forgot her graceful posture and studied expression of boredom and opened her mouth in the most unladylike manner.

Even the queen raised her eyebrows. 'Is this a practical joke, Lord Granville?'

'I would have been an even worse man than I used to be if it were, Your Majesty. I have come to you to ask that you give your consent to our match. I should have requested that before I requested her hand. Since I serve His Majesty and Miss Dudley serves you, it would have been proper.'

'You serve in rather different capacities unless my memory betrays me. You are the heir to an ancient title. Miss Dudley was called to serve me out of my daughters' exuberance over her writing, nothing more.'

Out of the corner of his eye, Hugh saw Lady Marianne snicker and Lavinia grow pale as though struck. It must have been quite something to hear the years of service she believed to be a thing of high honour and high duty reduced to this.

'Does it mean, Your Majesty, that you disapprove of the match?'

'Entirely so. For a viscount to marry a young woman without either a noble title to her name or a penny to her dowry is preposterous. I have no taste for the preposterous.'

'In that case,' Hugh replied, a kind of champagne-like, dangerous cheer rising within him, 'I will have to resign my post as His Majesty's equerry.'

In the ensuing silence, one could hear a fly buzzing on the wall.

'Do not go beyond the line from where you shall not be able to return, Lord Granville. Your nomination to the post has been my husband's decision, much against my advice on the matter. Should you be so foolish as to surrender this honour, you will never be able to recover it. Neither would your sons – or the sons of their sons – at our heir's court to come.'

Hugh had little doubt she would make sure of that. Whatever Queen Charlotte's habits were like, easily forgiving slights was not one of them, and this was exactly how she was likely to see it – as a slight against the benevolence she and her royal husband bestowed upon him.

He thought of the hours spent by his own father's side, listening to his wistful tales of the gilded court he was exiled from. It felt like a monstrous injustice back then, almost as though his father was a prince turned out of his kingdom and Hugh an heir of legend who would restore the Granvilles' rightful throne.

But what did this rightful throne at the true king's side amount to in the end? Hours of mindless boredom within four walls. Scores of vicious rumours traded as though they were currency. Layers of breathtaking pretence with their tableaux, their royal chapels, their promenades on the terrace and their ravings in the night.

Lavinia stood by his side, a bright bird with wings broken by servitude in this very gilded court his father had dreamed of until his death. His Lavinia.

Hugh drew in a long breath and exhaled slowly. 'In that case, my sons will have to live without it, much as I am going to love them. I would rather sacrifice their great honours than their very existence.'

'You made your choice, Lord Granville. I hope, for your sake, you do not come to rue this day when the attractions of your young bride will fade,' Queen Charlotte added.

There was something petty about this little cruelty; it was a twist of the knife one could expect from a vicious great-aunt, not something one would hear issued from atop the throne. But then, her throne, at present, was an armchair.

'How kind of you to worry on my behalf, Your Majesty. But, I assure you, no such regrets are possible, for the love I bear Miss Dudley has little dependence on the attractions of her youth.'

The ladies-in-waiting blanched as though he struck the royal personage instead of politely – outwardly so, at least – correcting her.

Lavinia did not quite smile. She had a temper too tightly controlled to do so in the presence of the woman who, until two minutes ago, had ruled her life. But the corners of her mouth softened almost imperceptibly.

It was a small change, the kind Hugh would have never noticed in any of the lovers who enjoyed his company before. The kind of change, he imagined, a novelist would notice with their eye for human expression and human folly. Perhaps, love indeed made artists of everyone.

The thought amused him, and when they left the drawing room temporarily hallowed by the royal presence with whispers at their back, he smiled.

The world around Lavinia seemed transformed. It was like the colours of sunset touching walls, painting them in riotous red, but it was morning, and every sober person would be going about their duties, ignorant about the great change.

The only duty left to her was to pack her belongings and prepare for their departure from court. Lavinia didn't bother with the slow, stately walk anymore. She raced down the corridors of Fauconberg Lodge as though a giddy girl who never knew fetters. At the landing of the small staircase that led to her room, she even stopped and laughed. She was free. She was finally free. Free and soon to get married to the man she loved most in all the world.

Her laughter was cut short when someone gripped her arm – viciously so, their fingers digging in. Lavinia spun around, her giddiness replaced by horror. An absurd thought raced through her head that, perhaps, the very walls of the royal court, the walls that went up around it wherever it went, were going to trap her in, never letting her escape into the green world outside.

But the face she saw was not that of some gothic fury. The face was that of Mrs Schwellenberg, the first keeper of the robes.

'You little schemer,' the older woman hissed. 'I was right after all. You did find yourself a protector.'

'In the most noble sense of the word,' Lavinia replied, her heart still beating madly from the combination of joy and residual fear. 'Not in the one you thought it to be.'

'I suspected you were setting your cap at the viscount. I should have stopped it at once, back when he made you that strange offer of accompanying him in his carriage.'

'I do wonder what right you would have had to do so, given that you are neither my parent nor my guardian.'

'I am the woman responsible for your performance of your duties here and for your moral conduct. You have neglected the former and disregarded the latter. Do not think that I had not noticed that your bed was undisturbed last night.'

'You went into my room?' Lavinia stiffened.

'I do so every morning.' Mrs Schwellenberg shrugged. 'How else am I to know you have not been getting up to some mischief? In this case, I was right. You have used every trick a young woman can employ to snare a good match, have you not? Let me tell you something I have learnt over decades of serving at this court – a promise does not a marriage make.

'Your viscount is not going to marry you now that he sampled your favours. No man would pay for what he can enjoy for free. When the next spring comes, you are not going to find yourself the mistress of Granville Hall – you are going to find yourself a mistress discarded. Don't crawl to me begging for me to employ my influence to get your honoured post back.'

Lavinia almost wanted to laugh again. She used to fear this woman as if she were an agent of divine wrath instead of a vicious harpy whose chief joy was making the lives of those below her station miserable. Well, it occurred to her, no deity could possibly fault her if she were to pay her tormentor in kind at least a little now.

'I am not going to crawl to you, Mrs Schwellenberg. On the contrary. I am going to be an honoured wife of the man I love and an author of novels that are going to flood the circulating libraries throughout the land. *You* are going to grow old and expire at this court. You will spend years going through the beds and drawers of young women in search of secrets more exciting than anything in your own life can possibly be.'

Mrs Schwellenberg raised her hand to slap her as though she were a disrespectful, impudent young girl.

Lavinia grabbed her wrist. 'You will not lay your hand on me,' Lavinia said, looking into her eyes, full of powerless rage as they were. 'You will not even lay a finger on me. You have no power over me now, Mrs Schwellenberg. I am going beyond this place, and you are not going to follow me there.'

'God forbid I follow you to the gutter where you are doubtless heading.'

'Then hear the last thing I am ever going to say to you. Pass it to whatever gossip you care. I would rather die in a gutter than live under your eye.'

Epilogue

'**S**ir Stephen seemed surprised,' Lady Lavinia Granville noted, sitting down on the lavish bed she shared with her husband.

'He just thought I was going to wed you much earlier,' Hugh replied, running his fingers lightly over the back of her neck, undoing her string of pearls.

'I see you are in one of your moods to play a maid to me,' Lavinia teased. She couldn't ignore the tingling the anticipation occasioned in her. 'But why would he have thought so?'

'He saw us in the upper assembly room in Cheltenham.'

'Our last trip? But... Oh, no, you mean the first time? When we had been engaged in that sordid charade with Miss Peabody?'

The former Miss Peabody had given the London papers more fodder than they knew what to do with. The conservative King-and-Country editors grumbled about the devious foreigners stealing the best Englishwomen away, but Lavinia never found out which criteria allowed them to rank Madeline among those best.

The newspapers of the more liberal persuasion praised Kurt von Wallmoden's petty potentate of a father for proving his generous views by accepting his younger son's marriage below his rank. That was the closest they could have ever come to overtly criticizing King George for the old sin of the Royal Marriages Act. When it was first signed, they could, and did, castigate him for a tyrant, but that was almost two decades ago and in peacetime. Now, even the boldest writer for the press had to be cautious.

'Just then.' Hugh's hand moved a little, and the freed necklace slid languidly over Lavinia's skin. She shivered slightly in a way that had little to do with the cold caress of the pearls. 'He thought you to be my betrothed then or at least a woman I intended to court.'

'I remember what you were like back then. Your friend Sir Stephen has a very vivid imagination.'

'Or, perhaps, he is just very perceptive,' Hugh parried, 'and noticed the way I was looking at you even back then. Like an artist notices. Or a writer.' His arm snaked out around Lavinia's waist, and he pulled her to him. She fell back against him, whimpered out of surprise, laughed, and whimpered again, recalling the cost of the gown of white satin with purple breast bows she had been wearing for tonight's ball and was wearing still.

'Be careful,' she said breathlessly. 'What if I stain or tear it?'

'Ever the careful housekeeper, aren't you?' Hugh placed a chaste kiss upon her forehead, then a far less chaste kiss upon her neck, and finally a completely unchaste one upon her mouth.

Lavinia responded without a thought, feeling his hands pressing, caressing, undressing. She giggled like a girl when she had to wriggle her arms out of the sleeves, then push the gown down.

It didn't take her long to shed her clothing completely. She did not wear the old-fashioned hoops of whalebone to support her petticoats now, the kind that had been de rigueur at court. When Lavinia first tried the simpler new fashions at the mischievous suggestion of her husband during their homebound honeymoon, she felt almost naked with only a shift between her petticoats and her skin. Hugh's very vocal appreciation helped her to get used to it, however, and now she rather delighted in the new freedom of movement.

She found it allowed her, among other things, to pace the study created for her in one of the guest bedrooms of Granville Hall very energetically when pondering some twist of her second novel's plot.

Art and commerce alike were very far from Lavinia's mind now, however, with Hugh devouring her with his eyes. She blushed a little as she stepped out of the shift pooling around her feet and knelt upon the bed.

'My Lavinia,' Hugh whispered, his hands settling upon her bare hips. 'My genius little wife.'

Did you like this story? If so, you might enjoy A Poetess and an Heir, the next installment in the series!